THE
LEGACY

ETERNITY NOW: VOLUME 1

THE LEGACY

MATTHEW
WRITER TO THE HEBREWS
JAMES
JUDE

www.ThomasNelson.com

NET NT Series Eternity Now: *Volume 1: The Legacy*

Copyright © 2022 by Thomas Nelson, a division of HarperCollins Christian Publishing, Inc.

Published in Nashville, Tennessee, by Thomas Nelson. Thomas Nelson is a registered trademark of HarperCollins Christian Publishing, Inc.

The NET Bible, New English Translation
Copyright © 1996, 2019 by Biblical Studies Press, LLC

NET Bible® is a registered trademark.

For free access to the NET Bible, the complete set of 60,000 translators' notes, and Bible study resources, visit:

bible.org
netbible.org

netbible.com

Used by permission. All rights reserved.

Library of Congress Control Number: 2021950933

This Bible was set in the Thomas Nelson NET Typeface, created at the 2K/DENMARK A/S type foundry.

All rights reserved.

Printed in the United States of America

23 24 25 25 27 28 29 30 / TRM / 10 9 8 7 6 5 4 3 2

CONTENTS

To the Reader: An Introduction to the New
English Translation vii

Matthew 1
Hebrews................................. 97
James................................... 129
Jude 141

TO THE READER

AN INTRODUCTION TO THE NEW ENGLISH TRANSLATION

You have been born anew ... through the living and enduring word of God.
1 Peter 1:23

The New English Translation (NET) is the newest complete translation of the original biblical languages into English. In 1995 a multidenominational team of more than twenty-five of the world's foremost biblical scholars gathered around the shared vision of creating an English Bible translation that could overcome old challenges and boldly open the door for new possibilities. The translators completed the first edition in 2001 and incorporated revisions based on scholarly and user feedback in 2003 and 2005. In 2019 a major update reached its final stages. The NET's unique translation process has yielded a beautiful, faithful English Bible for the worldwide church today.

What sets the NET Bible apart from other translations? We encourage you to read the full story of the NET's development and additional details about its translation philosophy at netbible.com/net-bible-preface. But we would like to draw your attention to a few features that commend the NET to all readers of the Word.

TRANSPARENT AND ACCOUNTABLE

Have you ever wished you could look over a Bible translator's shoulder as he or she worked?

Bible translation usually happens behind closed doors—few outside the translation committee see the complex decisions underlying the words that appear in their English Bibles. Fewer still have the opportunity to review and speak into the translators' decisions.

Throughout the NET's translation process, every working draft was made publicly available on the Internet. Bible scholars, ministers, and laypersons from around the world logged millions of review sessions. No other translation is so openly accountable to the worldwide church or has been so thoroughly vetted.

And yet the ultimate accountability was to the biblical text itself. The NET Bible is neither crowdsourced nor a "translation by consensus." Rather, the NET translators filtered every question and suggestion through the very best insights from biblical linguistics, textual criticism, and their unswerving commitment to following the text wherever it leads. Thus, the NET remains supremely accurate and trustworthy while also benefiting from extensive review by those who would be reading, studying, and teaching from its pages.

BEYOND THE "READABLE VS. ACCURATE" DIVIDE

The uniquely transparent and accountable translation process of the NET has been crystallized in the most extensive set of Bible translators' notes ever created. More than 60,000 notes highlight every major decision, outline alternative views, and explain difficult or nontraditional renderings. Freely available at netbible.org and in print in the *NET Bible, Full Notes Edition*, these notes help the NET overcome one of the biggest challenges facing any Bible translation: the tension between *accuracy* and *readability*.

If you have spent more than a few minutes researching the English version of the Bible, you have probably encountered a "translation spectrum"—a simple chart with the most wooden-but-precise translations and paraphrases on the far left (representing a "word-for-word" translation approach) and the loosest-but-easiest-to-read translations and paraphrases on the far right (representing a "thought-for-thought" philosophy of translation). Some translations intentionally lean toward one end of the spectrum or the other, embracing the strengths and weaknesses of their chosen approach. Most try to strike a balance between the extremes, weighing accuracy against readability—striving to reflect the grammar of the underlying biblical languages while still achieving acceptable English style.

But the NET moves beyond that old dichotomy. Because of the extensive translators' notes, the NET never has to compromise. Whenever faced with a difficult translation choice, the translators were free to put the strongest option in the main text while documenting the challenge, their thought process, and the solution in the notes.

The benefit to you, the reader? You can be sure that the NET is a translation you can trust—nothing has been lost in translation or obscured by a translator's dilemma. Instead, you are invited to see for yourself and gain the kind of transparent access to the biblical languages previously available only to scholars.

MINISTRY FIRST

One more reason to love the NET: Modern Bible translations are typically copyrighted, posing a challenge for ministries hoping to quote more than a few passages in their Bible study resources, curriculum, or other programming. But the NET is for everyone, with "ministry first" copyright innovations that encourage ministries to quote and share the life-changing message of Scripture as freely as possible. In fact, one of the major motivations behind the creation of the NET was the desire to ensure that ministries had unfettered access to a top-quality modern Bible translation without needing to embark on a complicated process of securing permissions.

Visit netbible.com/net-bible-copyright to learn more.

TAKE UP AND READ

With its balanced, easy-to-understand English text and a transparent translation process that invites you to see for yourself the richness of the biblical languages, the NET is a Bible you can embrace as your own. Clear, readable, elegant, and accurate, the NET presents Scripture as meaningfully and powerfully today as when these words were first communicated to the people of God.

Our prayer is that the NET will be a fresh and exciting invitation to you—and Bible readers everywhere—to "let the word of Christ dwell in you richly" (Col 3:16).

The Publishers

MATTHEW

PROLOGUE

Matthew lived as an outsider in his own land. Even something as simple as shopping in the town market brought sneers and insults from storekeepers and fellow customers alike. Every scornful word, gesture, and expression stung. He tried to ignore it all, but he couldn't. And no end was in sight.

Matthew lived as an outcast among his own people for one simple reason: he was a tax collector. The problem wasn't collecting taxes itself. It was how the taxes were taken and who the taxes went to. Matthew was allowed to take as much as he could get from people as long as Rome, Israel's occupying force, got its cut. His career was certainly lucrative, but it was self-serving. His fellow Jews held him in deserved contempt. To them, he was both a thief and a traitor.

But then one day, Matthew met a man who was different. This man didn't reject him. He didn't insult or mock him. The man *welcomed* him.

The man's name was Jesus. He was a traveling teacher, reportedly doing miracles and claiming to be the Messiah. Since his childhood Matthew had heard the stories of a Messiah who would rescue the Hebrews from oppression. For centuries the Jews had anticipated his arrival. Could this Jesus be the fulfillment of the ancient prophecies? One thing was sure: Jesus was shaking up Matthew's world with his claims and welcome to all people. And he is still doing that today.

CHAPTER 1

THE GENEALOGY OF JESUS CHRIST

This is the record of the genealogy of Jesus Christ, the son of David, the son of Abraham.

Abraham was the father of Isaac, Isaac the father of Jacob, Jacob the father of Judah and his brothers, Judah the father of Perez and Zerah (by Tamar), Perez the father of Hezron, Hezron the father of Ram, Ram the father of Amminadab, Amminadab the father of Nahshon, Nahshon the father of Salmon, Salmon the father of Boaz (by Rahab), Boaz the father of Obed (by Ruth), Obed the father of Jesse, and Jesse the father of David the king.

David was the father of Solomon (by the wife of Uriah), Solomon the father of Rehoboam, Rehoboam the father of Abijah, Abijah the father of Asa, Asa the father of Jehoshaphat, Jehoshaphat the father of Joram, Joram the father of Uzziah, Uzziah the father of Jotham, Jotham the father of Ahaz, Ahaz the father of Hezekiah, Hezekiah the father of Manasseh, Manasseh the father of Amon, Amon the father of Josiah, and Josiah the father of Jeconiah and his brothers, at the time of the deportation to Babylon.

After the deportation to Babylon, Jeconiah became the father of Shealtiel, Shealtiel the father of Zerubbabel, Zerubbabel the father of Abiud, Abiud the father of Eliakim, Eliakim the father of Azor, Azor the father of Zadok, Zadok the father of Achim, Achim the father of Eliud, Eliud the father of Eleazar, Eleazar the father of Matthan, Matthan the father of Jacob, and Jacob the father of Joseph, the husband of Mary, by whom Jesus was born, who is called Christ.

So all the generations from Abraham to David are fourteen generations, and from David to the deportation to Babylon, fourteen generations, and from the deportation to Babylon to Christ, fourteen generations.

THE BIRTH OF JESUS CHRIST

Now the birth of Jesus Christ happened this way. While his mother Mary was engaged to Joseph, but before they came together, she was found to be pregnant through the Holy Spirit. Because Joseph, her husband to be, was a righteous man, and because he did not want to disgrace her, he intended to divorce her privately. When he had contemplated this, an angel of the Lord appeared to him in a dream and said, "Joseph, son of David, do not be afraid to take Mary as your wife because the child conceived in her is from the Holy Spirit. She will give birth to a son and you will name him Jesus because he will save his people from their sins." This all happened so that what was spoken by the Lord through the prophet would be fulfilled: "*Look! The virgin will conceive and give birth to a son, and they will name him Emmanuel,*" which means "*God with us.*" When Joseph awoke from sleep he did what the angel of the Lord told him. He took his wife, but did not have marital relations with her until she gave birth to a son, whom he named Jesus.

CHAPTER 2

THE VISIT OF THE WISE MEN

After Jesus was born in Bethlehem in Judea, in the time of King Herod, wise men from the East came to Jerusalem saying, "Where is the one who is born king of the Jews? For we saw his star when it rose and have come to worship him." When King Herod heard this he was alarmed, and all Jerusalem with him. After assembling all the chief priests and experts in the law, he asked them where the Christ was to be born. "In Bethlehem of Judea," they said, "for it is written this way by the prophet:

'*And you, Bethlehem, in the land of Judah,*
are in no way least among the rulers of
Judah,
for out of you will come a ruler who will
shepherd my people Israel.' "

Then Herod privately summoned the wise men and determined from them when the star had appeared. He sent them to Bethlehem and said, "Go and look carefully for the child. When you find him, inform me so that I can go and worship him as well." After listening to the king they left, and once again the star they saw when it rose led them until it stopped above the place where the child was. When they saw the star they shouted joyfully. As they came into the house and saw the child with Mary his mother, they bowed down and worshiped him. They opened their treasure boxes and gave him gifts of gold, frankincense, and myrrh. After being warned in a dream not to return to Herod, they went back by another route to their own country.

THE ESCAPE TO EGYPT

After they had gone, an angel of the Lord appeared to Joseph in a dream and said, "Get up, take the child and his mother and flee to Egypt, and stay there until I tell you, for Herod is going to look for the child to kill him." Then he got up, took the child and his mother during the night, and went to Egypt. He stayed there until Herod died. In this way what was spoken by the Lord through the prophet was fulfilled: "*I called my Son out of Egypt.*"

When Herod saw that he had been tricked by the wise men, he became enraged. He sent men to kill all the children in Bethlehem and throughout the surrounding region from the age of two and under, according to the time he had learned from the wise men. Then what was spoken by Jeremiah the prophet was fulfilled:

"A voice was heard in Ramah,
weeping and loud wailing,
Rachel weeping for her children,
and she did not want to be comforted,
*   because they were gone."*

THE RETURN TO NAZARETH

After Herod had died, an angel of the Lord appeared in a dream to Joseph in Egypt saying, "Get up, take the child and his mother, and go to the land of Israel, for those who were seeking the child's life are dead." So he got up and took the child and his mother and returned to the land of Israel. But when he heard that Archelaus was reigning over Judea in place of his father Herod, he was afraid to go there. After being warned in a dream, he went to the regions of Galilee. He came to a town called Nazareth and lived there. Then what had been spoken by the prophets was fulfilled, that Jesus would be called a Nazarene.

CHAPTER 3

THE MINISTRY OF JOHN THE BAPTIST

In those days John the Baptist came into the wilderness of Judea proclaiming, "Repent, for the kingdom of heaven is near." For he is the one about whom the prophet Isaiah had spoken:

"The voice of one shouting in the wilderness,
'Prepare the way for the Lord, make his
paths straight.' "

Now John wore clothing made from camel's hair with a leather belt around his waist, and his diet consisted of locusts and wild honey. Then people from Jerusalem, as well as all Judea and all the region around the Jordan, were going out to him, and he was baptizing them in the Jordan River as they confessed their sins.

But when he saw many Pharisees and Sadducees coming to his baptism, he said to them, "You offspring of vipers! Who warned you to flee from the coming wrath? Therefore produce fruit that proves your repentance, and don't think you can say to yourselves, 'We have Abraham as our father.' For I tell you that God can raise up children for Abraham from these stones! Even now the ax is laid at the root of the trees, and every tree that does not produce good fruit will be cut down and thrown into the fire.

"I baptize you with water, for repentance, but the one coming after me is more powerful than I am—I am not worthy to carry his sandals! He will baptize you with the Holy Spirit and fire. His winnowing fork is in his hand, and he will clean out his threshing floor and will gather his wheat into the storehouse, but the chaff he will burn up with inextinguishable fire!"

THE BAPTISM OF JESUS

Then Jesus came from Galilee to John to be baptized by him in the Jordan River. But John tried to prevent him, saying, "I need to be baptized by you, and yet you come to me?" So Jesus replied to him, "Let it happen now, for it is right for us to fulfill all righteousness." Then John yielded to him. After Jesus was baptized, just as he was coming up out of the water, the heavens opened and he saw the Spirit of God descending like a dove and coming to rest on him. And a voice from heaven said, "This is my one dear Son; in him I take great delight."

CHAPTER 4

THE TEMPTATION OF JESUS

Then Jesus was led by the Spirit into the wilderness to be tempted by the devil. After he fasted 40 days and 40 nights he was famished. The tempter came and said to him, "If you are the Son of God, command these stones to become bread." But he answered, "It is written, *'Man does not live by bread alone, but by every word that comes from the mouth of God.'* " Then the devil took him to the holy city, had him stand on the highest point of the temple, and said to him, "If you are the Son of God, throw yourself down. For it is written, *'He will command his angels concerning you'* and *'with their hands they will lift you up, so that you will not strike your foot against a stone.'* " Jesus said to him, "Once again it is written:

'*You are not to put the Lord your God to the test.*'" Again, the devil took him to a very high mountain, and showed him all the kingdoms of the world and their grandeur. And he said to him, "I will give you all these things if you throw yourself to the ground and worship me." Then Jesus said to him, "Go away, Satan! For it is written: '*You are to worship the Lord your God and serve* only *him.*'" Then the devil left him, and angels came and began ministering to his needs.

PREACHING IN GALILEE

Now when Jesus heard that John had been imprisoned, he went into Galilee. While in Galilee, he moved from Nazareth to make his home in Capernaum by the sea, in the region of Zebulun and Naphtali, so that what was spoken by the prophet Isaiah would be fulfilled:

> "*Land of Zebulun and land of Naphtali,*
> *the way by the sea, beyond the Jordan,*
> *Galilee of the Gentiles—*
> *the people who sit in darkness have seen a*
> *great light,*
> *and on those who sit in the region and*
> *shadow of death a light has dawned.*"

From that time Jesus began to preach this message: "Repent, for the kingdom of heaven is near!"

THE CALL OF THE DISCIPLES

As he was walking by the Sea of Galilee he saw two brothers, Simon (called Peter) and Andrew his brother, casting a net into the sea (for they were fishermen). He said to them, "Follow me, and I will turn you into fishers of people!" They left their nets immediately and followed him. Going on from there he saw two other brothers, James the son of Zebedee and his brother John, in a boat with their father Zebedee, mending their nets. Then he called them. They immediately left the boat and their father and followed him.

JESUS' HEALING MINISTRY

Jesus went throughout all of Galilee, teaching in their synagogues, preaching the gospel of the kingdom, and healing every kind of disease and sickness among the people. So a report about him spread throughout Syria. People brought to him all who suffered with various illnesses and afflictions, those who had seizures, paralytics, and those possessed by demons, and he healed them. And large crowds followed him from Galilee, the Decapolis, Jerusalem, Judea, and beyond the Jordan River.

CHAPTER 5

THE BEATITUDES

When he saw the crowds, he went up the mountain. After he sat down his disciples came to him. Then he began to teach them by saying:

"Blessed are the poor in spirit, for the kingdom of heaven belongs to them.

Blessed are those who mourn, for they will be comforted.

Blessed are the meek, for they will inherit the earth.

Blessed are those who hunger and thirst for righteousness, for they will be satisfied.

Blessed are the merciful, for they will be shown mercy.

Blessed are the pure in heart, for they will see God.

Blessed are the peacemakers, for they will be called the children of God.

Blessed are those who are persecuted for righteousness, for the kingdom of heaven belongs to them.

Blessed are you when people insult you and persecute you and say all kinds of evil things about you falsely on account of me. Rejoice and be glad because your reward is great in heaven, for they persecuted the prophets before you in the same way.

SALT AND LIGHT

"You are the salt of the earth. But if salt loses its flavor, how can it be made salty again? It is no longer good for anything except to be thrown out and trampled on by people! You are the light of the world. A city located on a hill cannot be hidden. People do not light a lamp and put it under a basket but on a lampstand, and it gives light to all in the house. In the same way, let your light shine before people, so that they can see your good deeds and give honor to your Father in heaven.

FULFILLMENT OF THE LAW AND PROPHETS

"Do not think that I have come to abolish the law or the prophets. I have not come to abolish these things but to fulfill them. I tell you the truth, until heaven and earth pass away not the smallest letter or stroke of a letter will pass from the law until everything takes place. So anyone who breaks one of the least of these commands and teaches others to do so will be called least in the kingdom of heaven, but whoever obeys them and teaches others to do so will be called great in the kingdom of heaven. For I tell you, unless your righteousness goes beyond that of the experts in the law and the Pharisees, you will never enter the kingdom of heaven!

ANGER AND MURDER

"You have heard that it was said to an older generation, '*Do not murder*,' and 'whoever murders will be subjected to judgment.' But I say to you that anyone who is angry with a brother will be subjected to judgment. And whoever insults a brother will be brought before the council, and whoever says 'Fool' will be sent to fiery hell. So then, if you bring your gift to the altar and there you remember that your brother has something against you, leave your gift there in front of the altar. First go and be reconciled to your brother and then come and present your gift. Reach agreement quickly with your accuser while on the way to court, or he may hand you over to the judge, and the judge hand you over to the warden, and you will be thrown into prison. I tell you the truth, you will never get out of there until you have paid the last penny!

ADULTERY

"You have heard that it was said, *'Do not commit adultery.'* But I say to you that whoever looks at a woman to desire her has already committed adultery with her in his heart. If your right eye causes you to sin, tear it out and throw it away! It is better to lose one of your members than to have your whole body thrown into hell. If your right hand causes you to sin, cut it off and throw it away! It is better to lose one of your members than to have your whole body go into hell.

DIVORCE

"It was said, *'Whoever divorces his wife must give her a legal document.'* But I say to you that everyone who divorces his wife, except for immorality, makes her commit adultery, and whoever marries a divorced woman commits adultery.

OATHS

"Again, you have heard that it was said to an older generation, '*Do not break an oath, but fulfill your vows to the Lord.*' But I say to you, do not take oaths at all—not by heaven because it is the throne of God, not by earth because it is his footstool, and not by Jerusalem because it is the city of the great King. Do not take an oath by your head because you are not able to make one hair white or black. Let your word be 'Yes, yes' or 'No, no.' More than this is from the evil one.

RETALIATION

"You have heard that it was said, '*An eye for an eye and a tooth for a tooth.*' But I say to you, do not resist the evildoer. But whoever strikes you on the right cheek, turn the other to him as well. And if someone wants to sue you and take your tunic, let him have your coat also. And if anyone forces you to go one mile, go with him two. Give to the one who asks you, and do not reject the one who wants to borrow from you.

LOVE FOR ENEMIES

"You have heard that it was said, '*Love your neighbor*' and 'hate your enemy.' But I say to you, love your enemy and pray for those who persecute you, so that you may be like your Father in heaven, since he causes the sun to rise on the evil and the good, and sends rain on the righteous and the unrighteous. For if you love those who love you, what reward do you have? Even the tax collectors do the same, don't they? And if you only greet your brothers, what more do you do? Even the Gentiles do the same, don't they? So then, be perfect, as your heavenly Father is perfect.

CHAPTER 6

PURE-HEARTED GIVING

"Be careful not to display your righteousness merely to be seen by people. Otherwise you have no reward with your Father in heaven. Thus whenever you do charitable giving, do not blow a trumpet before you, as the hypocrites do in synagogues and on streets so that people will praise them. I tell you the truth, they have their reward! But when you do your giving, do not let your left hand know what your right hand is doing, so that your gift may be in secret. And your Father, who sees in secret, will reward you.

PRIVATE PRAYER

"Whenever you pray, do not be like the hypocrites because they love to pray while standing in synagogues and on street corners so that people can see them. Truly I say to you, they have their reward! But whenever you pray, go into your inner room, close the door, and pray to your Father in secret. And your Father, who sees in secret, will reward you. When you pray, do not babble repetitiously like the Gentiles because they think that by their many words they will be heard. Do not be like them, for your Father knows what you need before you ask him. So pray this way:

> "Our Father in heaven, may your name
> be honored,
> may your kingdom come,
> may your will be done on earth as it is in
> heaven.
> Give us today our daily bread,
> and forgive us our debts, as we ourselves
> have forgiven our debtors.
> And do not lead us into temptation, but
> deliver us from the evil one.

"For if you forgive others their sins, your heavenly Father will also forgive you. But if you do not forgive others, your Father will not forgive you your sins.

PROPER FASTING

"When you fast, do not look sullen like the hypocrites, for they make their faces unattractive so that people will see them fasting. I tell you the truth, they have their reward! When you fast, anoint your head and wash your face, so that it will not be obvious to others when you are fasting, but only to your Father who is in secret. And your Father, who sees in secret, will reward you.

LASTING TREASURE

"Do not accumulate for yourselves treasures on earth, where moth and devouring insect destroy and where thieves break in and steal. But accumulate for yourselves treasures in heaven, where moth and devouring insect do not destroy, and thieves do not break in and steal. For where your treasure is, there your heart will be also.

"The eye is the lamp of the body. If then your eye is healthy, your whole body will be full of light. But if your eye is diseased, your whole body will be full of darkness. If then the light in you is darkness, how great is the darkness!

"No one can serve two masters, for either he will hate the one and love the other, or he will be devoted to the one and despise the other. You cannot serve God and money.

DO NOT WORRY

"Therefore I tell you, do not worry about your life, what you will eat or drink, or about your body, what you will wear. Isn't there more to life than food and more to the body than clothing? Look at the birds in the sky: They do not sow, or reap, or gather into barns, yet your heavenly Father feeds them. Aren't you more valuable than they are? And which of you by worrying can add even one hour to his life? Why do you worry about clothing? Think about how the flowers of the field grow; they do not work or spin. Yet I tell you that not even Solomon in all his glory was clothed like one of these! And if this is how God clothes the wild grass, which is here today and tomorrow is tossed into the fire to heat the oven, won't he clothe you even more, you people of little faith? So then, don't worry saying, 'What will we eat?' or 'What will we drink?' or 'What will we wear?' For the un-converted pursue these things, and your heavenly Father knows that you need them. But above all pursue his kingdom and righteousness, and all these things will be given to you as well. So then, do not worry about tomorrow, for tomorrow will worry about itself. Today has enough trouble of its own.

CHAPTER 7

DO NOT JUDGE

"Do not judge so that you will not be judged. For by the standard you judge you will be judged, and the measure you use will be the measure you receive. Why do you see the speck in your brother's eye, but fail to see the beam of wood in your own? Or how can you say to your brother, 'Let me remove the speck from your eye,' while there is a beam in your own? You hypocrite! First remove the beam from your own eye, and then you can see clearly to remove the speck from your brother's eye. Do not give what is holy to dogs or throw your pearls before pigs; otherwise they will trample them under their feet and turn around and tear you to pieces.

ASK, SEEK, KNOCK

"Ask and it will be given to you; seek and you will find; knock and the door will be opened for you. For everyone who asks receives, and the one who seeks finds, and to the one who knocks, the door will be opened. Is there anyone among you who, if his son asks for bread, will give him a stone? Or if he asks for a fish, will give him a snake? If you then, although you are evil, know how to give good gifts to your children, how much more will your Father in heaven give good gifts to those who ask him! In everything, treat others as you would want them to treat you, for this fulfills the law and the prophets.

THE NARROW GATE

"Enter through the narrow gate because the gate is wide and the way is spacious that leads to destruction, and there are many who enter through it. How narrow is the gate and difficult the way that leads to life, and there are few who find it!

A TREE AND ITS FRUIT

"Watch out for false prophets, who come to you in sheep's clothing but inwardly are voracious wolves. You will recognize them by their fruit. Grapes are not gathered from thorns or figs from thistles, are they? In the same way, every good tree bears good fruit, but the bad tree bears bad fruit. A good tree is not able to bear bad fruit, nor a bad tree to bear good fruit. Every tree that does not bear good fruit is cut down and thrown into the fire. So then, you will recognize them by their fruit.

JUDGMENT OF PRETENDERS

"Not everyone who says to me, 'Lord, Lord,' will enter into the kingdom of heaven—only the one who does the will of my Father in heaven. On that day, many will say to me, 'Lord, Lord, didn't we prophesy in your name, and cast out demons in your name, and do many powerful deeds in your name?' Then I will declare to them, 'I never knew you. Go away from me, you lawbreakers!'

HEARING AND DOING

"Everyone who hears these words of mine and does them is like a wise man who built his house on rock. The rain fell, the flood came, and the winds beat against that house, but it did not collapse because its foundation had been laid on rock. Everyone who hears these words of mine and does not do them is like a foolish man who built his house on sand. The rain fell, the flood came, and the winds beat against that house, and it collapsed—it was utterly destroyed!"

When Jesus finished saying these things, the crowds were amazed by his teaching, because he taught them like one who had authority, not like their experts in the law.

CHAPTER 8

CLEANSING A LEPER

After he came down from the mountain, large crowds followed him. And a leper approached and bowed low before him, saying, "Lord, if you are willing, you can make me clean." He stretched out his hand and touched him saying, "I am willing. Be clean!" Immediately his leprosy was cleansed. Then Jesus said to him, "See that you do not speak to anyone, but go, show yourself to the priest, and bring the offering that Moses commanded, as a testimony to them."

HEALING THE CENTURION'S SERVANT

When he entered Capernaum, a centurion came to him asking for help: "Lord, my servant is lying at home paralyzed, in terrible anguish." Jesus said to him, "I will come and heal him." But the centurion replied, "Lord, I am not worthy to have you come under my roof! Instead, just say the word and my servant will be healed. For I too am a man under authority, with soldiers under me. I say to this one, 'Go!' and he goes, and to another 'Come!' and he comes, and to my slave 'Do this!' and he does it." When Jesus heard this he was amazed and said to those who followed him, "I tell you the truth, I have not found such faith in anyone in Israel! I tell you, many will come from the east and west to share the banquet with Abraham, Isaac, and Jacob in the kingdom of heaven, but the sons of the kingdom will be thrown out into the outer darkness, where there will be weeping and gnashing of teeth." Then Jesus said to the centurion, "Go; just as you believed, it will be done for you." And the servant was healed at that hour.

HEALINGS AT PETER'S HOUSE

Now when Jesus entered Peter's house, he saw his mother-in-law lying down, sick with a fever. He touched her hand, and the fever left her. Then she got up and began to serve them. When it was evening, many demon-possessed people were brought to him. He drove out the spirits with a word, and healed all who were sick. In this way what was spoken by the prophet Isaiah was fulfilled:

"He took our weaknesses and carried our diseases."

CHALLENGING PROFESSED FOLLOWERS

Now when Jesus saw a large crowd around him, he gave orders to go to the other side of the lake. Then an expert in the law came to him and said, "Teacher, I will follow you wherever you go." Jesus said to him, "Foxes have dens, and the birds in the sky have nests, but the Son of Man has no place to lay his head." Another of the disciples said to him, "Lord, let me first go and bury my father." But Jesus said to him, "Follow me, and let the dead bury their own dead."

STILLING OF A STORM

As he got into the boat, his disciples followed him. And a great storm developed on the sea so that the waves began to swamp the boat. But he was asleep. So they came and woke him up saying, "Lord, save us! We are about to die!" But he said to them, "Why are you cowardly, you people of little faith?" Then he got up and rebuked the winds and the sea, and it was dead calm. And the men were amazed and said, "What sort of person is this? Even the winds and the sea obey him!"

HEALING THE GADARENE DEMONIACS

When he came to the other side, to the region of the Gadarenes, two demon-possessed men coming from the tombs met him. They were extremely violent, so that no one was able to pass by that way. They cried out, "Son of God, leave us alone! Have you come here to torment us before the time?" A large herd of pigs was feeding some distance from them. Then the demons begged him, "If you drive us out, send us into the herd of pigs." And he said, "Go!" So they came out and went into the pigs, and the herd rushed down the steep slope into the lake and drowned in the water. The herdsmen ran off, went into the town, and told everything that had happened to the demon-possessed men. Then the entire town came out to meet Jesus. And when they saw him, they begged him to leave their region.

CHAPTER 9

HEALING AND FORGIVING A PARALYTIC

After getting into a boat he crossed to the other side and came to his own town. Just then some people brought to him a paralytic lying on a stretcher. When Jesus saw their faith, he said to the paralytic, "Have courage, son! Your sins are forgiven." Then some of the experts in the law said to themselves, "This man is blaspheming!" When Jesus perceived their thoughts he said, "Why do you respond with evil in your hearts? Which is easier, to say, 'Your sins are forgiven' or to say, 'Stand up and walk'? But so that you may know that the Son of Man has authority on earth to forgive sins"—then he said to the paralytic—"Stand up, take your stretcher, and go home." So he stood up and went home. When the crowd saw this, they were afraid and honored God who had given such authority to men.

THE CALL OF MATTHEW;
EATING WITH SINNERS

As Jesus went on from there, he saw a man named Matthew sitting at the tax booth. "Follow me," he said to him. So he got up and followed him. As Jesus was having a meal in Matthew's house, many tax collectors and sinners came and ate with Jesus and his disciples. When the Pharisees saw this they said to his disciples, "Why does your teacher eat with tax collectors and sinners?" When Jesus heard this he said, "Those who are healthy don't need a physician, but those who are sick do. Go and learn what this saying means: *'I want mercy and not sacrifice.'* For I did not come to call the righteous, but sinners."

THE SUPERIORITY OF THE NEW

Then John's disciples came to Jesus and asked, "Why do we and the Pharisees fast often, but your disciples don't fast?" Jesus said to them, "The wedding guests cannot mourn while the bridegroom is with them, can they? But the days are coming when the bridegroom will be taken from them, and then they will fast. No one sews a patch of unshrunk cloth on an old garment because the patch will pull away from the garment and the tear will be worse. And no one pours new wine into old wineskins; otherwise the skins burst and the wine is spilled out and the skins are destroyed. Instead they put new wine into new wineskins and both are preserved."

RESTORATION AND HEALING

As he was saying these things, a leader came, bowed low before him, and said, "My daughter has just died, but come and lay your hand on her and she will live." Jesus and his disciples got up and followed him. But a woman who had been suffering from a hemorrhage for 12 years came up behind him and touched the edge of his cloak. For she kept saying to herself, "If only I touch his cloak, I will be healed." But when Jesus turned and saw her he said, "Have courage, daughter! Your faith has made you well." And the woman was healed from that hour. When Jesus entered the leader's house and saw the flute players and the disorderly crowd, he said, "Go away, for the girl is not dead but asleep!" And they began making fun of him. But when the crowd had been forced outside, he went in and gently took her by the hand, and the girl got up. And the news of this spread throughout that region.

HEALING THE BLIND AND MUTE

As Jesus went on from there, two blind men began to follow him, shouting, "Have mercy on us, Son of David!" When he went into the house, the blind men came to him. Jesus said to them, "Do you believe that I am able to do this?" They said to him, "Yes, Lord." Then he touched their eyes saying, "Let it be done for you according to your faith." And their eyes were opened. Then Jesus sternly warned them, "See that no one knows about this!" But they went out and spread the news about him throughout that entire region.

As they were going away, a man who was demon-possessed and unable to speak was brought to him. After the demon was cast out, the man who had been mute began to speak. The crowds were amazed and said, "Never has anything like this been seen in Israel!" But the Pharisees said, "By the ruler of demons he casts out demons!"

WORKERS FOR THE HARVEST

Then Jesus went throughout all the towns and villages, teaching in their synagogues, preaching the good news of the kingdom, and healing every kind of disease and sickness.

When he saw the crowds, he had compassion on them because they were bewildered and helpless, like sheep without a shepherd. Then he said to his disciples, "The harvest is plentiful, but the workers are few. Therefore ask the Lord of the harvest to send out workers into his harvest-ready fields."

CHAPTER 10

SENDING OUT THE 12 APOSTLES

Jesus called his twelve disciples and gave them authority over unclean spirits so they could cast them out and heal every kind of disease and sickness. Now these are the names of the 12 apostles: first, Simon (called Peter), and Andrew his brother; James son of Zebedee and John his brother; Philip and Bartholomew; Thomas and Matthew the tax collector; James the son of Alphaeus, and Thaddaeus; Simon the Zealot and Judas Iscariot, who betrayed him.

Jesus sent out these 12, instructing them as follows: "Do not go on a road that leads to Gentile regions and do not enter any Samaritan town. Go instead to the lost sheep of the house of Israel. As you go, preach this message: 'The kingdom of heaven is near!' Heal the sick, raise the dead, cleanse lepers, cast out demons. Freely you received, freely give. Do not take gold, silver, or copper in your belts; no bag for the journey; or an extra tunic or sandals or staff; for the worker deserves his provisions. Whenever you enter a town or village, find out who is worthy there and stay with them until you leave. As you enter the house, greet those within it. And if the house is worthy, let your peace come on it, but if it is not worthy, let your peace return to you. And if anyone will not welcome you or listen to your message, shake the dust off your feet as you leave that house or that town. I tell you the truth, it will be more bearable for the region of Sodom and Gomorrah on the day of judgment than for that town!

PERSECUTION OF DISCIPLES

"I am sending you out like sheep surrounded by wolves, so be wise as serpents and innocent as doves. Beware of people, because they will hand you over to councils and flog you in their synagogues. And you will be brought before governors and kings because of me, as a witness to them and to the Gentiles. Whenever they hand you over for trial, do not worry about how to speak or what to say, for what you should say will be given to you at that time. For it is not you speaking, but the Spirit of your Father speaking through you.

"Brother will hand over brother to death, and a father his child. Children will rise against parents and have them put to death. And you will be hated by everyone because of my name. But the one who endures to the end will be saved! Whenever they persecute you in one town, flee to another! I tell you the truth, you will not finish going through all the towns of Israel before the Son of Man comes.

"A disciple is not greater than his teacher, nor a slave greater than his master. It is enough for the disciple to become like his teacher, and the slave like his master. If they have called the head of the house 'Beelzebul,' how much worse will they call the members of his household!

FEAR GOD, NOT MAN

"Do not be afraid of them, for nothing is hidden that will not be revealed, and nothing is secret that will not be made known. What I say to you in the dark, tell in the light, and what is whispered in your ear, proclaim from the housetops. Do not be afraid of those who kill the body but cannot kill the soul. Instead, fear the one who is able to destroy both soul and body in hell. Aren't two sparrows sold for a penny? Yet not one of them falls to the ground apart from your Father's will. Even all the hairs on your head are numbered. So do not be afraid; you are more valuable than many sparrows.

"Whoever, then, acknowledges me before people, I will acknowledge before my Father in heaven. But whoever denies me before people, I will deny him also before my Father in heaven.

NOT PEACE, BUT A SWORD

"Do not think that I have come to bring peace to the earth. I have not come to bring peace but a sword! For I have come to set *a man against his father, a daughter against her mother, and a daughter-in-law against her mother-in-law, and a man's enemies will be the members of his household.*

"Whoever loves father or mother more than me is not worthy of me, and whoever loves son or daughter more than me is not worthy of me. And whoever does not take up his cross and follow me is not worthy of me. Whoever finds his life will lose it, and whoever loses his life because of me will find it.

REWARDS

"Whoever receives you receives me, and whoever receives me receives the one who sent me. Whoever receives a prophet in the name of a prophet will receive a prophet's reward. Whoever receives a righteous person in the name of a righteous person will receive a righteous person's reward. And whoever gives only a cup of cold water to one of these little ones in the name of a disciple, I tell you the truth, he will never lose his reward."

CHAPTER 11

When Jesus had finished instructing his 12 disciples, he went on from there to teach and preach in their towns.

JESUS AND JOHN THE BAPTIST

Now when John heard in prison about the deeds Christ had done, he sent his disciples to ask a question: "Are you the one who is to come, or should we look for another?" Jesus answered them, "Go tell John what you hear and see: The blind see, the lame walk, lepers are cleansed, the deaf hear, the dead are raised, and the poor have good news proclaimed to them —and blessed is anyone who takes no offense at me!"

While they were going away, Jesus began to speak to the crowd about John: "What did you go out into the wilderness to see? A reed shaken by the wind? What did you go out to see? A man dressed in soft clothing? Look, those who wear soft clothing are in the palaces of kings! What did you go out to see? A prophet? Yes, I tell you, and more than a prophet! This is the one about whom it is written:

" *'Look, I am sending my messenger ahead*
of you,
who will prepare your way before you.'

"I tell you the truth, among those born of women, no one has arisen greater than John the Baptist. Yet the one who is least in the kingdom of heaven is greater than he is! From the days of John the Baptist until now the kingdom of heaven has suffered violence, and forceful people lay hold of it. For all the prophets and the law prophesied until John appeared. And if you are willing to accept it, he is Elijah, who is to come. The one who has ears had better listen!

"To what should I compare this generation? They are like children sitting in the market-places who call out to one another,

> " 'We played the flute for you, yet you did
> not dance;
> we wailed in mourning, yet you did not
> weep.'

For John came neither eating nor drinking, and they say, 'He has a demon!' The Son of Man came eating and drinking, and they say, 'Look at him, a glutton and a drunk, a friend of tax collectors and sinners!' But wisdom is vindicated by her deeds."

WOES ON UNREPENTANT CITIES

Then Jesus began to criticize openly the cities in which he had done many of his miracles because they did not repent. "Woe to you, Chorazin! Woe to you, Bethsaida! If the miracles done in you had been done in Tyre and Sidon, they would have repented long ago in sackcloth and ashes. But I tell you, it will be more bearable for Tyre and Sidon on the day of judgment than for you! And you, Capernaum, will you be exalted to heaven? No, you will be thrown down to Hades! For if the miracles done among you had been done in Sodom, it would have continued to this day. But I tell you, it will be more bearable for the region of Sodom on the day of judgment than for you!"

JESUS' INVITATION

At that time Jesus said, "I praise you, Father, Lord of heaven and earth, because you have hidden these things from the wise and intelligent, and have revealed them to little children. Yes, Father, for this was your gracious will. All things have been handed over to me by my Father. No one knows the Son except the Father, and no one knows the Father except the Son and anyone to whom the Son decides to reveal him. Come to me, all you who are weary and burdened, and I will give you rest. Take my yoke on you and learn from me because I am gentle and humble in heart, and you will find rest for your souls. For my yoke is easy to bear, and my load is not hard to carry."

CHAPTER 12

LORD OF THE SABBATH

At that time Jesus went through the grain fields on a Sabbath. His disciples were hungry, and they began to pick heads of wheat and eat them. But when the Pharisees saw this they said to him, "Look, your disciples are doing what is against the law to do on the Sabbath." He said to them, "Haven't you read what David did when he and his companions were hungry—how he entered the house of God and ate the sacred bread, which was against the law for him or his companions to eat, but only for the priests? Or have you not read in the law that the priests in the temple desecrate the Sabbath and yet are not guilty? I tell you that something greater than the temple is here. If you had known what this means: *'I want mercy and not sacrifice,'* you would not have condemned the innocent. For the Son of Man is lord of the Sabbath."

Then Jesus left that place and entered their synagogue. A man was there who had a withered hand. And they asked Jesus, "Is it lawful to heal on the Sabbath?" so that they could accuse him. He said to them, "Would not any one of you, if he had one sheep that fell into a pit on the Sabbath, take hold of it and lift it out? How much more valuable is a person than a sheep! So it is lawful to do good on the Sabbath." Then he said to the man, "Stretch out your hand." He stretched it out and it was restored, as healthy as the other. But the Pharisees went out and plotted against him, as to how they could assassinate him.

GOD'S SPECIAL SERVANT

Now when Jesus learned of this, he went away from there. Great crowds followed him, and he healed them all. But he sternly warned them not to make him known. This fulfilled what was spoken by the prophet Isaiah:

"Here is my servant whom I have chosen,
the one I love, in whom I take great delight.
I will put my Spirit on him, and he will
proclaim justice to the nations.
He will not quarrel or cry out,

nor will anyone hear his voice in the
  streets.
He will not break a bruised reed or
  extinguish a smoldering wick,
until he brings justice to victory.
And in his name the Gentiles will hope."

JESUS AND BEELZEBUL

Then they brought to him a demon-possessed man who was blind and mute. Jesus healed him so that he could speak and see. All the crowds were amazed and said, "Could this one be the Son of David?" But when the Pharisees heard this they said, "He does not cast out demons except by the power of Beelzebul, the ruler of demons!" Now when Jesus realized what they were thinking, he said to them, "Every kingdom divided against itself is destroyed, and no town or house divided against itself will stand. So if Satan casts out Satan, he is divided against himself. How then will his kingdom stand? And if I cast out demons by Beelzebul, by whom do your sons cast them out? For this reason they will be your judges. But if I cast out demons by the Spirit of God, then the kingdom of God has already overtaken you. How else can someone enter a strong man's house and steal his property, unless he first ties up the strong man? Then he can thoroughly plunder the house. Whoever is not with me is against me, and whoever does not gather with me scatters. For this reason I tell you, people will be forgiven for every sin and blasphemy, but the blasphemy against the Spirit will not be forgiven. Whoever speaks a word against the Son of Man will be forgiven. But whoever speaks against the Holy Spirit will not be forgiven, either in this age or in the age to come.

TREES AND THEIR FRUIT

"Make a tree good and its fruit will be good, or make a tree bad and its fruit will be bad, for a tree is known by its fruit. Offspring of vipers! How are you able to say anything good, since you are evil? For the mouth speaks from what fills the heart. The good person brings good things out of his good treasury, and the evil person brings evil things out of his evil treasury. I tell you that on the day of judgment, people will give an account for every worthless word they speak. For by your words you will be justified, and by your words you will be condemned."

THE SIGN OF JONAH

Then some of the experts in the law along with some Pharisees answered him, "Teacher, we want to see a sign from you." But he answered them, "An evil and adulterous generation asks for a sign, but no sign will be given to it except the sign of the prophet Jonah. For just as Jonah was *in the belly of the huge fish for three days and three nights,* so the Son of Man will be in the heart of the earth for three days and three nights. The people of Nineveh will stand up at the judgment with this generation and condemn it because they repented when Jonah preached to them—and now, something greater than Jonah is here! The queen of the South will rise up at the judgment with this generation and condemn it because she came from the ends of the earth to hear the wisdom of Solomon—and now, something greater than Solomon is here!

THE RETURN OF THE UNCLEAN SPIRIT

"When an unclean spirit goes out of a person, it passes through waterless places looking for rest but does not find it. Then it says, 'I will return to the home I left.' When it returns, it finds the house empty, swept clean, and put in order. Then it goes and brings with it seven other spirits more evil than itself, and they go in and live there, so the last state of that person is worse than the first. It will be that way for this evil generation as well!"

JESUS' TRUE FAMILY

While Jesus was still speaking to the crowds, his mother and brothers came and stood outside, asking to speak to him. Someone told him, "Look, your mother and your brothers are standing outside wanting to speak to you." To the one who had said this, Jesus replied, "Who is my mother and who are my brothers?" And pointing toward his disciples he said, "Here are my mother and my brothers! For whoever does the will of my Father in heaven is my brother and sister and mother."

CHAPTER 13

THE PARABLE OF THE SOWER

On that day after Jesus went out of the house, he sat by the lake. And such a large crowd gathered around him that he got into a boat to sit while the whole crowd stood on the shore. He told them many things in parables, saying: "Listen! A sower went out to sow. And as he sowed, some seeds fell along the path, and the birds came and devoured them. Other seeds fell on rocky ground where they did not have much soil. They sprang up quickly because the soil was not deep. But when the sun came up, they were scorched, and because they did not have sufficient root, they withered. Other seeds fell among the thorns, and they grew up and choked them. But other seeds fell on good soil and produced grain, some a hundred times as much, some sixty, and some thirty. The one who has ears had better listen!"

Then the disciples came to him and said, "Why do you speak to them in parables?" He replied, "You have been given the opportunity to know the secrets of the kingdom of heaven, but they have not. For whoever has will be given more, and will have an abundance. But whoever does not have, even what he has will be taken from him. For this reason I speak to them in parables: Although they see they do not see, and although they hear they do not hear nor do they understand.

And concerning them the prophecy of Isaiah is fulfilled that says:

> " 'You will listen carefully yet will never understand,
> you will look closely yet will never comprehend.
> For the heart of this people has become dull;
> they are hard of hearing,
> and they have shut their eyes,
> so that they would not see with their eyes
> and hear with their ears
> and understand with their hearts
> and turn, and I would heal them.'

"But your eyes are blessed because they see, and your ears because they hear. For I tell you the truth, many prophets and righteous people longed to see what you see but did not see it, and to hear what you hear but did not hear it.

"So listen to the parable of the sower: When anyone hears the word about the kingdom and does not understand it, the evil one comes and snatches what was sown in his heart; this is the seed sown along the path. The seed sown on rocky ground is the person who hears the word and immediately receives it with joy. But he has no root in himself and does not endure; when trouble or persecution comes because of the word, immediately he falls away. The seed sown among thorns is the person who hears the word, but worldly cares and the seductiveness of wealth choke the word, so it produces nothing. But as for the seed sown on good soil, this is the person who hears the word and understands. He bears fruit, yielding a hundred, sixty, or thirty times what was sown."

THE PARABLE OF THE WEEDS

He presented them with another parable: "The kingdom of heaven is like a person who sowed good seed in his field. But while everyone was sleeping, an enemy came and sowed darnel among the wheat and went away. When the plants sprouted and produced grain, then the darnel also appeared. So the slaves of the landowner came and said to him, 'Sir, didn't you sow good seed in your field? Then where did the darnel come from?' He said, 'An enemy has done this!' So the slaves replied, 'Do you want us to go and gather it?' But he said, 'No, since in gathering the darnel you may uproot the wheat along with it. Let both grow together until the harvest. At harvest time I will tell the reapers, "First collect the darnel and tie it in bundles to be burned, but then gather the wheat into my barn." ' "

THE PARABLE OF THE MUSTARD SEED

He gave them another parable: "The kingdom of heaven is like a mustard seed that a man took and sowed in his field. It is the smallest of all the seeds, but when it has grown it is the greatest garden plant and becomes a tree, so that the wild birds come and nest in its branches."

THE PARABLE OF THE YEAST

He told them another parable: "The kingdom of heaven is like yeast that a woman took and mixed with three measures of flour until all the dough had risen."

THE PURPOSE OF PARABLES

Jesus spoke all these things in parables to the crowds; he did not speak to them without a parable. This fulfilled what was spoken by the prophet:

"I will open my mouth in parables,
I will announce what has been hidden
from the foundation of the world."

EXPLANATION FOR THE DISCIPLES

Then he left the crowds and went into the house. And his disciples came to him saying, "Explain to us the parable of the darnel in the field." He answered, "The one who sowed the good seed is the Son of Man. The field is the world and the good seed are the people of the kingdom. The poisonous weeds are the people of the evil one, and the enemy who sows them is the devil. The harvest is the end of the age, and the reapers are angels. As the poisonous weeds are collected and burned with fire, so it will be at the end of the age. The Son of Man will send his angels, and they will gather from his kingdom everything that causes sin as well as all lawbreakers. They will *throw them into the fiery furnace,* where there will be weeping and gnashing of teeth. Then *the righteous will shine like the sun in the kingdom of their Father.* The one who has ears had better listen!

PARABLES ON THE KINGDOM OF HEAVEN

"The kingdom of heaven is like a treasure, hidden in a field, that a person found and hid. Then because of joy he went and sold all that he had and bought that field.

"Again, the kingdom of heaven is like a merchant searching for fine pearls. When he found a pearl of great value, he went out and sold everything he had and bought it.

"Again, the kingdom of heaven is like a net that was cast into the sea that caught all kinds of fish. When it was full, they pulled it ashore, sat down, and put the good fish into containers and threw the bad away. It will be this way at the end of the age. Angels will come and separate the evil from the righteous and *throw them into the fiery furnace,* where there will be weeping and gnashing of teeth.

"Have you understood all these things?" They replied, "Yes." Then he said to them, "Therefore every expert in the law who has been trained for the kingdom of heaven is like the owner of a house who brings out of his treasure what is new and old."

REJECTION AT NAZARETH

Now when Jesus finished these parables, he moved on from there. Then he came to his hometown and began to teach the people in their synagogue. They were astonished and said, "Where did this man get such wisdom and miraculous powers? Isn't this the carpenter's son? Isn't his mother named Mary? And aren't his brothers James, Joseph, Simon, and Judas? And aren't all his sisters here with us? So where did he get all this?" And so they took offense at him. But Jesus said to them, "A prophet is not without honor except in his hometown and in his own house." And he did not do many miracles there because of their unbelief.

CHAPTER 14

THE DEATH OF JOHN THE BAPTIST

At that time Herod the tetrarch heard reports about Jesus, and he said to his servants, "This is John the Baptist. He has been raised from the dead! And because of this, miraculous powers are at work in him." For Herod had arrested John, bound him, and put him in prison on account of Herodias, his brother Philip's wife, because John had repeatedly told him, "It is not lawful for you to have her." Although Herod wanted to kill John, he feared the crowd because they accepted John as a prophet. But on Herod's birthday, the daughter of Herodias danced before them and pleased Herod, so much that he promised with an oath to give her whatever she asked. Instructed by her mother, she said, "Give me the head of John the Baptist here on a platter." Although it grieved the king because of his oath and the dinner guests, he commanded it to be given. So he sent and had John beheaded in the prison. His head was brought on a platter and given to the girl, and she brought it to her mother. Then John's disciples came and took the body and buried it and went and told Jesus.

THE FEEDING OF THE 5,000

Now when Jesus heard this he went away from there privately in a boat to an isolated place. But when the crowd heard about it, they followed him on foot from the towns. As he got out he saw the large crowd, and he had compassion on them and healed their sick. When evening arrived, his disciples came to him saying, "This is an isolated place and the hour is already late. Send the crowds away so that they can go into the villages and buy food for themselves." But he replied, "They don't need to go. You give them something to eat." They said to him, "We have here only five loaves and two fish." "Bring them here to me," he replied. Then he instructed the crowds to sit down on the grass. He took the five loaves and two fish, and looking up to heaven he gave thanks and broke the loaves. He gave them to the disciples, who in turn gave them to the crowds. They all ate and were satisfied, and they picked up the broken pieces left over, 12 baskets full. Not counting women and children, there were about 5,000 men who ate.

WALKING ON WATER

Immediately Jesus made the disciples get into the boat and go ahead of him to the other side, while he dispersed the crowds. And after he sent the crowds away, he went up the mountain by himself to pray. When evening came, he was there alone. Meanwhile the boat, already far from land, was taking a beating from the waves because the wind was against it. As the night was ending, Jesus came to them walking on the sea. When the disciples saw him walking on the water they were terrified and said, "It's a ghost!" and cried out with fear. But immediately Jesus spoke to them: "Have courage! It is I. Do not be afraid." Peter said to him, "Lord, if it is you, order me to come to you on the water." So he said, "Come." Peter got out of the boat, walked on the water, and came toward Jesus. But when he saw the strong wind he became afraid. And starting to sink, he cried out, "Lord, save me!" Immediately Jesus reached out his hand and caught him, saying to him, "You of little faith, why did you doubt?" When they went up into the boat, the wind ceased. Then those who were in the boat worshiped him, saying, "Truly you are the Son of God."

After they had crossed over, they came to land at Gennesaret. When the people there recognized him, they sent word into all the surrounding area, and they brought all their sick to him. They begged him if they could only touch the edge of his cloak, and all who touched it were healed.

CHAPTER 15

BREAKING HUMAN TRADITIONS

Then Pharisees and experts in the law came from Jerusalem to Jesus and said, "Why do your disciples disobey the tradition of the elders? For they don't wash their hands when they eat." He answered them, "And why do you disobey the commandment of God because of your tradition? For God said, '*Honor your father and mother*' and '*Whoever insults his father or mother must be put to death.*' But you say, 'If someone tells his father or mother, "Whatever help you would have received from me is given to God," he does not need to honor his father.' You have nullified the word of God on account of your tradition. Hypocrites! Isaiah prophesied correctly about you when he said,

"'*This people honors me with their lips,*
but their hearts are far from me,
and they worship me in vain,
teaching as doctrines the commandments of men.'"

TRUE DEFILEMENT

Then he called the crowd to him and said, "Listen and understand. What defiles a person is not what goes into the mouth; it is what comes out of the mouth that defiles a person." Then the disciples came to him and said, "Do you know that when the Pharisees heard this saying they were offended?" And he replied, "Every plant that my heavenly Father did not plant will be uprooted. Leave them! They are blind guides. If someone who is blind leads another who is blind, both will fall into a pit." But Peter said to him, "Explain this parable to us." Jesus said, "Even after all this, are you still so foolish? Don't you understand that whatever goes into the mouth enters the stomach and then passes out into the sewer? But the things that come out of the mouth come from the heart, and these things defile a person. For out of the heart come evil ideas, murder, adultery, sexual immorality, theft, false testimony, slander. These are the things that defile a person; it is not eating with unwashed hands that defiles a person."

A CANAANITE WOMAN'S FAITH

After going out from there, Jesus went to the region of Tyre and Sidon. A Canaanite woman from that area came and cried out, "Have mercy on me, Lord, Son of David! My daughter is horribly demon-possessed!" But he did not answer her a word. Then his disciples came and begged him, "Send her away because she keeps on crying out after us." So he answered, "I was sent only to the lost sheep of the house of Israel." But she came and bowed down before him and said, "Lord, help me!" "It is not right to take the children's bread and throw it to the dogs," he said. "Yes, Lord," she replied, "but even the dogs eat the crumbs that fall from their masters' table."

Then Jesus answered her, "Woman, your faith is great! Let what you want be done for you." And her daughter was healed from that hour.

HEALING MANY OTHERS

When he left there, Jesus went along the Sea of Galilee. Then he went up a mountain, where he sat down. Then large crowds came to him bringing with them the lame, blind, crippled, mute, and many others. They laid them at his feet, and he healed them. As a result, the crowd was amazed when they saw the mute speaking, the crippled healthy, the lame walking, and the blind seeing, and they praised the God of Israel.

THE FEEDING OF THE 4,000

Then Jesus called his disciples and said, "I have compassion on the crowd because they have already been here with me three days and they have nothing to eat. I don't want to send them away hungry since they may faint on the way." The disciples said to him, "Where can we get enough bread in this desolate place to satisfy so great a crowd?" Jesus said to them, "How many loaves do you have?" They replied, "Seven—and a few small fish." After instructing the crowd to sit down on the ground, he took the seven loaves and the fish, and after giving thanks, he broke them and began giving them to the disciples, who then gave them to the crowds. They all ate and were satisfied, and they picked up the broken pieces left over, seven baskets full. Not counting children and women, there were 4,000 men who ate. After sending away the crowd, he got into the boat and went to the region of Magadan.

CHAPTER 16

THE DEMAND FOR A SIGN

Now when the Pharisees and Sadducees came to test Jesus, they asked him to show them a sign from heaven. He said, "When evening comes you say, 'It will be fair weather because the sky is red,' and in the morning, 'It will be stormy today because the sky is red and darkening.' You know how to judge correctly the appearance of the sky, but you cannot evaluate the signs of the times. A wicked and adulterous generation asks for a sign, but no sign will be given to it except the sign of Jonah." Then he left them and went away.

THE YEAST OF THE PHARISEES AND SADDUCEES

When the disciples went to the other side, they forgot to take bread. "Watch out," Jesus said to them, "beware of the yeast of the Pharisees and Sadducees." So they began to discuss this among themselves, saying, "It is because we brought no bread." When Jesus learned of this, he said, "You who have such little faith! Why are you arguing among yourselves about having no bread? Do you still not understand?

Don't you remember the five loaves for the 5,000, and how many baskets you took up? Or the seven loaves for the 4,000 and how many baskets you took up? How could you not understand that I was not speaking to you about bread? But beware of the yeast of the Pharisees and Sadducees!" Then they understood that he had not told them to be on guard against the yeast in bread, but against the teaching of the Pharisees and Sadducees.

PETER'S CONFESSION

When Jesus came to the area of Caesarea Philippi, he asked his disciples, "Who do people say that the Son of Man is?" They answered, "Some say John the Baptist, others Elijah, and others Jeremiah or one of the prophets." He said to them, "But who do you say that I am?" Simon Peter answered, "You are the Christ, the Son of the living God." And Jesus answered him, "You are blessed, Simon son of Jonah, because flesh and blood did not reveal this to you, but my Father in heaven! And I tell you that you are Peter, and on this rock I will build my church, and the gates of Hades will not overpower it. I will give you the keys of the kingdom of heaven. Whatever you bind on earth will have been bound in heaven, and whatever you release on earth will have been released in heaven." Then he instructed his disciples not to tell anyone that he was the Christ.

FIRST PREDICTION OF JESUS' DEATH AND RESURRECTION

From that time on Jesus began to show his disciples that he must go to Jerusalem and suffer many things at the hands of the elders, chief priests, and experts in the law, and be killed and on the third day be raised. So Peter took him aside and began to rebuke him: "God forbid, Lord! This must not happen to you!" But he turned and said to Peter, "Get behind me, Satan! You are a stumbling block to me because you are not setting your mind on God's interests, but on man's." Then Jesus said to his disciples, "If anyone wants to become my follower, he must deny himself, take up his cross, and follow me. For whoever wants to save his life will lose it, but whoever loses his life because of me will find it. For what does it benefit a person if he gains the whole world but forfeits his life? Or what can a person give in exchange for his life? For the Son of Man will come with his angels in the glory of his Father, and then *he will reward each person according to what he has done.* I tell you the truth, there are some standing here who will not experience death before they see the Son of Man coming in his kingdom."

CHAPTER 17

THE TRANSFIGURATION

Six days later Jesus took with him Peter, James, and John the brother of James, and led them privately up a high mountain. And he was transfigured before them. His face shone like the sun, and his clothes became white as light. Then Moses and Elijah also appeared before them, talking with him. So Peter said to Jesus, "Lord, it is good for us to be here. If you want, I will make three shelters—one for you, one for Moses, and one for Elijah." While he was still speaking, a bright cloud overshadowed them, and a voice from the cloud said, "This is my one dear Son, in whom I take great delight. Listen to him!" When the disciples heard this, they were overwhelmed with fear and threw themselves down with their faces to the ground. But Jesus came and touched them. "Get up," he said. "Do not be afraid." When they looked up, all they saw was Jesus alone.

As they were coming down from the mountain, Jesus commanded them, "Do not tell anyone about the vision until the Son of Man is raised from the dead." The disciples asked him, "Why then do the experts in the law say that Elijah must come first?" He answered, "Elijah does indeed come first and will restore all things. And I tell you that Elijah has already come. Yet they did not recognize him, but did to him whatever they wanted. In the same way, the Son of Man will suffer at their hands." Then the disciples understood that he was speaking to them about John the Baptist.

THE DISCIPLES' FAILURE TO HEAL

When they came to the crowd, a man came to him, knelt before him, and said, "Lord, have mercy on my son because he has seizures and suffers terribly, for he often falls into the fire and into the water. I brought him to your disciples, but they were not able to heal him." Jesus answered, "You unbelieving and perverse generation! How much longer must I be with you? How much longer must I endure you? Bring him here to me." Then Jesus rebuked the demon and it came out of him, and the boy was healed from that moment. Then the disciples came to Jesus privately and said, "Why couldn't we cast it out?" He told them, "It was because of your little faith. I tell you the truth, if you have faith the size of a mustard seed, you will say to this mountain, 'Move from here to there,' and it will move; nothing will be impossible for you."

SECOND PREDICTION OF JESUS' DEATH AND RESURRECTION

When they gathered together in Galilee, Jesus told them, "The Son of Man is going to be betrayed into the hands of men. They will kill him, and on the third day he will be raised." And they became greatly distressed.

THE TEMPLE TAX

After they arrived in Capernaum, the collectors of the temple tax came to Peter and said, "Your teacher pays the double drachma tax, doesn't he?" He said, "Yes." When Peter came into the house, Jesus spoke to him first, "What do you think, Simon? From whom do earthly kings collect tolls or taxes—from their sons or from foreigners?" After he said, "From foreigners," Jesus said to him, "Then the sons are free. But so that we don't offend them, go to the lake and throw out a hook. Take the first fish that comes up, and when you open its mouth, you will find a four-drachma coin. Take that and give it to them for me and you."

CHAPTER 18

QUESTIONS ABOUT THE GREATEST

At that time the disciples came to Jesus saying, "Who is the greatest in the kingdom of heaven?" He called a child, had him stand among them, and said, "I tell you the truth, unless you turn around and become like little children, you will never enter the kingdom of heaven! Whoever then humbles himself like this little child is the greatest in the kingdom of heaven. And whoever welcomes a child like this in my name welcomes me.

"But if anyone causes one of these little ones who believe in me to sin, it would be better for him to have a huge millstone hung around his neck and to be drowned in the open sea. Woe to the world because of stumbling blocks! It is necessary that stumbling blocks come, but woe to the person through whom they come. If your hand or your foot causes you to sin, cut it off and throw it away. It is better for you to enter life crippled or lame than to have two hands or two feet and be thrown into eternal fire. And if your eye causes you to sin, tear it out and throw it away. It is better for you to enter into life with one eye than to have two eyes and be thrown into fiery hell.

THE PARABLE OF THE LOST SHEEP

"See that you do not disdain one of these little ones. For I tell you that their angels in heaven always see the face of my Father in heaven. What do you think? If someone owns a hundred sheep and one of them goes astray, will he not leave the ninety-nine on the mountains and go look for the one that went astray? And if he finds it, I tell you the truth, he will rejoice more over it than over the ninety-nine that did not go astray. In the same way, your Father in heaven is not willing that one of these little ones be lost.

RESTORING CHRISTIAN RELATIONSHIPS

"If your brother sins, go and show him his fault when the two of you are alone. If he listens to you, you have regained your brother. But if he does not listen, take one or two others with you, so that *at the testimony of two or three witnesses every matter may be established.* If he refuses to listen to them, tell it to the church. If he refuses to listen to the church, treat him like a Gentile or a tax collector.

"I tell you the truth, whatever you bind on earth will have been bound in heaven, and whatever you release on earth will have been released in heaven. Again, I tell you the truth, if two of you on earth agree about whatever you ask, my Father in heaven will do it for you. For where two or three are assembled in my name, I am there among them."

Then Peter came to him and said, "Lord, how many times must I forgive my brother who sins against me? As many as seven times?" Jesus said to him, "Not seven times, I tell you, but seventy-seven times!

THE PARABLE OF THE UNFORGIVING SLAVE

"For this reason, the kingdom of heaven is like a king who wanted to settle accounts with his slaves. As he began settling his accounts, a man who owed 10,000 talents was brought to him. Because he was not able to repay it, the lord ordered him to be sold, along with his wife, children, and whatever he possessed, and repayment to be made. Then the slave threw himself to the ground before him, saying, 'Be patient with me, and I will repay you everything.' The lord had compassion on that slave and released him, and forgave him the debt. After he went out, that same slave found one of his fellow slaves who owed him 100 silver coins. So he grabbed him by the throat and started to choke him, saying, 'Pay back what you owe me!' Then his fellow slave threw himself down and begged him,

'Be patient with me, and I will repay you.' But he refused. Instead, he went out and threw him in prison until he repaid the debt. When his fellow slaves saw what had happened, they were very upset and went and told their lord everything that had taken place. Then his lord called the first slave and said to him, 'Evil slave! I forgave you all that debt because you begged me! Should you not have shown mercy to your fellow slave, just as I showed it to you?' And in anger his lord turned him over to the prison guards to torture him until he repaid all he owed. So also my heavenly Father will do to you, if each of you does not forgive your brother from your heart."

CHAPTER 19

QUESTIONS ABOUT DIVORCE

Now when Jesus finished these sayings, he left Galilee and went to the region of Judea beyond the Jordan River. Large crowds followed him, and he healed them there.

Then some Pharisees came to him in order to test him. They asked, "Is it lawful to divorce a wife for any cause?" He answered, "Have you not read that from the beginning the Creator *made them male and female,* and said, '*For this reason a man will leave his father and mother and will be united with his wife, and the two will become one flesh*'? So they are no longer two, but one flesh. Therefore what God has joined together, let no one separate."

They said to him, "Why then did Moses command us *to give **a certificate of dismissal** and to divorce* her?" Jesus said to them, "Moses permitted you to divorce your wives because of your hard hearts, but from the beginning it was not this way. Now I say to you that whoever divorces his wife, except for immorality, and marries another commits adultery." The disciples said to him, "If this is the case of a husband with a wife, it is better not to marry!" He said to them, "Not everyone can accept this statement, except those to whom it has been given. For there are some eunuchs who were that way from birth, and some who were made eunuchs by others, and some who became eunuchs for the sake of the kingdom of heaven. The one who is able to accept this should accept it."

JESUS AND LITTLE CHILDREN

Then little children were brought to him for him to lay his hands on them and pray. But the disciples scolded those who brought them. But Jesus said, "Let the little children come to me and do not try to stop them, for the kingdom of heaven belongs to such as these." And he placed his hands on them and went on his way.

THE RICH YOUNG MAN

Now someone came up to him and said, "Teacher, what good thing must I do to gain eternal life?" He said to him, "Why do you ask me about what is good? There is only one who is good. But if you want to enter into life, keep the commandments." "Which ones?" he asked. Jesus replied, *"Do not murder, do not commit adultery, do not steal, do not give false testimony, honor your father and mother,* and *love your neighbor as yourself."* The young man said to him, "I have wholeheartedly obeyed all these laws. What do I still lack?" Jesus said to him, "If you wish to be perfect, go sell your possessions and give the money to the poor, and you will have treasure in heaven. Then come, follow me." But when the young man heard this he went away sorrowful, for he was very rich.

Then Jesus said to his disciples, "I tell you the truth, it will be hard for a rich person to enter the kingdom of heaven! Again I say, it is easier for a camel to go through the eye of a needle than for a rich person to enter into the kingdom of God." The disciples were greatly astonished when they heard this and said, "Then who can be saved?" Jesus looked at them and replied, "This is impossible for mere humans, but for God all things are possible." Then Peter said to him, "Look, we have left everything to follow you! What then will there be for us?" Jesus said to them, "I tell you the truth: In the age when all things are renewed, when the Son of Man sits on his glorious throne, you who have followed me will also sit on 12 thrones, judging the 12 tribes of Israel. And whoever has left houses or brothers or sisters or father or mother or children or fields for my sake will receive a hundred times as much and will inherit eternal life. But many who are first will be last, and the last first.

CHAPTER 20

WORKERS IN THE VINEYARD

"For the kingdom of heaven is like a landowner who went out early in the morning to hire workers for his vineyard. And after agreeing with the workers for the standard wage, he sent them into his vineyard. When it was about nine o'clock in the morning, he went out again and saw others standing around in the marketplace without work. He said to them, 'You go into the vineyard too, and I will give you whatever is right.' So they went. When he went out again about noon and three o'clock that afternoon, he did the same thing. And about five o'clock that afternoon he went out and found others standing around, and said to them, 'Why are you standing here all day without work?' They said to him, 'Because no one hired us.' He said to them, 'You go and work in the vineyard too.' When it was evening the owner of the vineyard said to his manager, 'Call the workers and pay them their wages starting with the last hired until the first.' When those hired about five o'clock came, each received a full day's pay. And when those hired first came, they thought they would receive more. But each one also received the standard wage. When they received it, they began to complain against the landowner, saying, 'These last fellows worked one hour, and you have made them equal to us who bore the hardship and burning heat of the day.' And the landowner replied to one of them, 'Friend, I am not treating you unfairly. Didn't you agree with me to work for the standard wage? Take what is yours and go. I want to give to this last man the same as I gave to you. Am I not permitted to do what I want with what belongs to me? Or are you envious because I am generous?' So the last will be first, and the first last."

THIRD PREDICTION OF JESUS' DEATH AND RESURRECTION

As Jesus was going up to Jerusalem, he took the twelve aside privately and said to them on the way, "Look, we are going up to Jerusalem, and the Son of Man will be handed over to the chief priests and the experts in the law. They will condemn him to death, and will turn him over to the Gentiles to be mocked and flogged severely and crucified. Yet on the third day, he will be raised."

A REQUEST FOR JAMES AND JOHN

Then the mother of the sons of Zebedee came to him with her sons, and kneeling down she asked him for a favor. He said to her, "What do you want?" She replied, "Permit these two sons of mine to sit, one at your right hand and one at your left, in your kingdom." Jesus answered, "You don't know what you are asking! Are you able to drink the cup I am about to drink?" They said to him, "We are able." He told them, "You will drink my cup, but to sit at my right and at my left is not mine to give. Rather, it is for those for whom it has been prepared by my Father."

Now when the other 10 heard this, they were angry with the two brothers. But Jesus called them and said, "You know that the rulers of the Gentiles lord it over them, and those in high positions use their authority over them. It must not be this way among you! Instead whoever wants to be great among you must be your servant, and whoever wants to be first among you must be your slave—just as the Son of Man did not come to be served but to serve, and to give his life as a ransom for many."

TWO BLIND MEN HEALED

As they were leaving Jericho, a large crowd followed them. Two blind men were sitting by the road. When they heard that Jesus was passing by, they shouted, "Have mercy on us, Lord, Son of David!" The crowd scolded them to get them to be quiet. But they shouted even more loudly, "Lord, have mercy on us, Son of David!" Jesus stopped, called them, and said, "What do you want me to do for you?" They said to him, "Lord, let our eyes be opened."

Moved with compassion, Jesus touched their eyes. Immediately they received their sight and followed him.

CHAPTER 21

THE TRIUMPHAL ENTRY

Now when they approached Jerusalem and came to Bethphage, at the Mount of Olives, Jesus sent two disciples, telling them, "Go to the village ahead of you. Right away you will find a donkey tied there, and a colt with her. Untie them and bring them to me. If anyone says anything to you, you are to say, 'The Lord needs them,' and he will send them at once." This took place to fulfill what was spoken by the prophet:

"Tell the people of Zion,
'Look, your king is coming to you,
unassuming and seated on a donkey,
and on a colt, the foal of a donkey.'"

So the disciples went and did as Jesus had instructed them. They brought the donkey and the colt and placed their cloaks on them, and he sat on them. A very large crowd spread their cloaks on the road. Others cut branches from the trees and spread them on the road. The crowds that went ahead of him and those following kept shouting, "*Hosanna* to the Son of David! *Blessed is the one who comes in the name of the Lord! Hosanna* in the highest!" As he entered Jerusalem the whole city was thrown into an uproar, saying, "Who is this?" And the crowds were saying, "This is the prophet Jesus, from Nazareth in Galilee."

CLEANSING THE TEMPLE

Then Jesus entered the temple area and drove out all those who were selling and buying in the temple courts and turned over the tables of the money changers and the chairs of those selling doves. And he said to them, "It is written, *'My house will be called a house of prayer,'* but you are turning it into *a den of robbers!*"

The blind and lame came to him in the temple courts, and he healed them. But when the chief priests and the experts in the law saw the wonderful things he did and heard the children crying out in the temple courts, "Hosanna to the Son of David," they became indignant and said to him, "Do you hear what they are saying?" Jesus said to them, "Yes. Have you never read, *'Out of the mouths of children and nursing infants you have prepared praise for yourself'*?" And leaving them, he went out of the city to Bethany and spent the night there.

THE WITHERED FIG TREE

Now early in the morning, as he returned to the city, he was hungry. After noticing a fig tree by the road he went to it, but found nothing on it except leaves. He said to it, "Never again will there be fruit from you!" And the fig tree withered at once. When the disciples saw it they were amazed, saying, "How did the fig tree wither so quickly?" Jesus answered them, "I tell you the truth, if you have faith and do not doubt, not only will you do what was done to the fig tree, but even if you say to this mountain, 'Be lifted up and thrown into the sea,' it will happen. And whatever you ask in prayer, if you believe, you will receive."

THE AUTHORITY OF JESUS

Now after Jesus entered the temple courts, the chief priests and elders of the people came up to him as he was teaching and said, "By what authority are you doing these things, and who gave you this authority?" Jesus answered them, "I will also ask you one question. If you answer me then I will also tell you by what authority I do these things. Where did John's baptism come from? From heaven or from people?" They discussed this among themselves, saying, "If we say, 'From heaven,' he will say, 'Then why did you not believe him?' But if we say, 'From people,' we fear the crowd, for they all consider John to be a prophet." So they answered Jesus, "We don't know." Then he said to them, "Neither will I tell you by what authority I am doing these things.

THE PARABLE OF THE TWO SONS

"What do you think? A man had two sons. He went to the first and said, 'Son, go and work in the vineyard today.' The boy answered, 'I will not.' But later he had a change of heart and went. The father went to the other son and said the same thing. This boy answered, 'I will, sir,' but did not go. Which of the two did his father's will?" They said, "The first." Jesus said to them, "I tell you the truth, tax collectors and prostitutes will go ahead of you into the kingdom of God! For John came to you in the way of righteousness, and you did not believe him. But the tax collectors and prostitutes did believe. Although you saw this, you did not later change your minds and believe him.

THE PARABLE OF THE TENANTS

"Listen to another parable: There was a landowner who planted a vineyard. He put a fence around it, dug a pit for its winepress, and built a watchtower. Then he leased it to tenant farmers and went on a journey. When the harvest time was near, he sent his slaves to the tenants to collect his portion of the crop. But the tenants seized his slaves, beat one, killed another, and stoned another. Again he sent other slaves, more than the first, and they treated them the same way. Finally he sent his son to them, saying, 'They will respect my son.' But when the tenants saw the son, they said to themselves, 'This is the heir. Come, let's kill him and get his inheritance!' So they seized him, threw him out of the vineyard, and killed him. Now when the owner of the vineyard comes, what will he do to those tenants?" They said to him, "He will utterly destroy those evil men! Then he will lease the vineyard to other tenants who will give him his portion at the harvest."

Jesus said to them, "Have you never read in the scriptures:

> " *'The stone the builders rejected has*
> *become the cornerstone.*
> *This is from the Lord, and it is marvelous*
> *in our eyes'*?

"For this reason I tell you that the kingdom of God will be taken from you and given to a people who will produce its fruit. The one who falls on this stone will be broken to pieces, and the one on whom it falls will be crushed." When the chief priests and the Pharisees heard his parables, they realized that he was speaking about them. They wanted to arrest him, but they were afraid of the crowds because the crowds regarded him as a prophet.

CHAPTER 22

THE PARABLE OF THE WEDDING BANQUET

Jesus spoke to them again in parables, saying: "The kingdom of heaven can be compared to a king who gave a wedding banquet for his son. He sent his slaves to summon those who had been invited to the banquet, but they would not come. Again he sent other slaves, saying, 'Tell those who have been invited, "Look! The feast I have prepared for you is ready. My oxen and fattened cattle have been slaughtered, and everything is ready. Come to the wedding banquet." ' But they were indifferent and went away, one to his farm, another to his business. The rest seized his slaves, insolently mistreated them, and killed them. The king was furious! He sent his soldiers, and they put those murderers to death and set their city on fire. Then he said to his slaves, 'The wedding is ready, but the ones who had been invited were not worthy. So go into the main streets and invite everyone you find to the wedding banquet.' And those slaves went out into the streets and gathered all they found, both bad and good, and the wedding hall was filled with guests. But when the king came in to see the wedding guests, he saw a man there who was not wearing wedding clothes. And he said to him, 'Friend, how did you get in here without wedding clothes?' But he had nothing to say. Then the king said to his attendants, 'Tie him up hand and foot and throw him into the outer darkness, where there will be weeping and gnashing of teeth!' For many are called, but few are chosen."

PAYING TAXES TO CAESAR

Then the Pharisees went out and planned together to entrap him with his own words. They sent to him their disciples along with the Herodians, saying, "Teacher, we know that you are truthful and teach the way of God in accordance with the truth. You do not court anyone's favor because you show no partiality. Tell us then, what do you think? Is it right to pay taxes to Caesar or not?"

But Jesus realized their evil intentions and said, "Hypocrites! Why are you testing me? Show me the coin used for the tax." So they brought him a denarius. Jesus said to them, "Whose image is this, and whose inscription?" They replied, "Caesar's." He said to them, "Then give to Caesar the things that are Caesar's, and to God the things that are God's." Now when they heard this they were stunned, and they left him and went away.

MARRIAGE AND THE RESURRECTION

The same day Sadducees (who say there is no resurrection) came to him and asked him, "Teacher, Moses said, *'If a man dies without having children, his brother must marry the widow and father children for his brother.'* Now there were seven brothers among us. The first one married and died, and since he had no children he left his wife to his brother. The second did the same, and the third, down to the seventh. Last of all, the woman died. In the resurrection, therefore, whose wife of the seven will she be? For they all had married her." Jesus answered them, "You are deceived because you don't know the scriptures or the power of God. For in the resurrection they neither marry nor are given in marriage, but are like angels in heaven. Now as for the resurrection of the dead, have you not read what was spoken to you by God, '*I am the God of Abraham, the God of Isaac, and the God of Jacob*'? He is not the God of the dead but of the living!" When the crowds heard this, they were amazed at his teaching.

THE GREATEST COMMANDMENT

Now when the Pharisees heard that he had silenced the Sadducees, they assembled together. And one of them, an expert in religious law, asked him a question to test him: "Teacher, which commandment in the law is the greatest?" Jesus said to him, " '*Love the Lord your God with all your heart, with all your soul, and with all your mind.*' This is the first and greatest commandment. The second is like it: '*Love your neighbor as yourself.*' All the law and the prophets depend on these two commandments."

THE MESSIAH: DAVID'S SON AND LORD

While the Pharisees were assembled, Jesus asked them a question: "What do you think about the Christ? Whose son is he?" They said, "The son of David." He said to them, "How then does David by the Spirit call him 'Lord,' saying,

" '*The Lord said to my lord,*
"*Sit at my right hand,*
 until I put your enemies under your feet" '?
If David then calls him 'Lord,' how can he be his son?" No one was able to answer him a word, and from that day on no one dared to question him any longer.

CHAPTER 23

SEVEN WOES

Then Jesus said to the crowds and to his disciples, "The experts in the law and the Pharisees sit on Moses' seat. Therefore pay attention to what they tell you and do it. But do not do what they do, for they do not practice what they teach. They tie up heavy loads, hard to carry, and put them on men's shoulders, but they themselves are not willing even to lift a finger to move them. They do all their deeds to be seen by people, for they make their phylacteries wide and their tassels long. They love the place of honor at banquets and the best seats in the synagogues and elaborate greetings in the marketplaces and to have people call them 'Rabbi.' But you are not to be called 'Rabbi,' for you have one Teacher and you are all brothers. And call no one your 'father' on earth, for you have one Father, who is in heaven. Nor are you to be called 'teacher,' for you have one Teacher, the Christ. The greatest among you will be your servant. And whoever exalts himself will be humbled, and whoever humbles himself will be exalted.

"But woe to you, experts in the law and you Pharisees, hypocrites! You keep locking people out of the kingdom of heaven! For you neither enter nor permit those trying to enter to go in.

"Woe to you, experts in the law and you Pharisees, hypocrites! You cross land and sea to make one convert, and when you get one, you make him twice as much a child of hell as yourselves!

"Woe to you, blind guides, who say, 'Whoever swears by the temple is bound by nothing. But whoever swears by the gold of the temple is bound by the oath.' Blind fools! Which is greater, the gold or the temple that makes the gold sacred? And, 'Whoever swears by the altar is bound by nothing. But if anyone swears by the gift on it he is bound by the oath.' You are blind! For which is greater, the gift or the altar that makes the gift sacred? So whoever swears by the altar swears by it and by everything on it. And whoever swears by the temple swears by it and the one who dwells in it. And whoever swears by heaven swears by the throne of God and the one who sits on it.

"Woe to you, experts in the law and you Pharisees, hypocrites! You give a tenth of mint, dill, and cumin, yet you neglect what is more important in the law—justice, mercy, and faithfulness! You should have done these things without neglecting the others. Blind guides! You strain out a gnat yet swallow a camel!

"Woe to you, experts in the law and you Pharisees, hypocrites! You clean the outside of the cup and the dish, but inside they are full of greed and self-indulgence. Blind Pharisee! First clean the inside of the cup, so that the outside may become clean too!

"Woe to you, experts in the law and you Pharisees, hypocrites! You are like white-washed tombs that look beautiful on the outside but inside are full of the bones of the dead and of everything unclean. In the same way, on the outside you look righteous to people, but inside you are full of hypocrisy and lawlessness.

"Woe to you, experts in the law and you Pharisees, hypocrites! You build tombs for the prophets and decorate the graves of the righteous. And you say, 'If we had lived in the days of our ancestors, we would not have participated with them in shedding the blood of the prophets.' By saying this you testify against yourselves that you are descendants of those who murdered the prophets. Fill up then the measure of your ancestors! You snakes, you offspring of vipers! How will you escape being condemned to hell?

"For this reason I am sending you prophets and wise men and experts in the law, some of whom you will kill and crucify, and some you will flog in your synagogues and pursue from town to town, so that on you will come all the righteous blood shed on earth, from the blood of righteous Abel to the blood of Zechariah son of Barachiah, whom you murdered between the temple and the altar. I tell you the truth, this generation will be held responsible for all these things!

JUDGMENT ON ISRAEL

"O Jerusalem, Jerusalem, you who kill the prophets and stone those who are sent to you! How often I have longed to gather your children together as a hen gathers her chicks under her wings, but you would have none of it! Look, your house is left to you desolate! For I tell you, you will not see me from now until you say, '*Blessed is the one who comes in the name of the Lord!*' "

CHAPTER 24

THE DESTRUCTION OF THE TEMPLE

Now as Jesus was going out of the temple courts and walking away, his disciples came to show him the temple buildings. And he said to them, "Do you see all these things? I tell you the truth, not one stone will be left on another. All will be torn down!"

SIGNS OF THE END OF THE AGE

As he was sitting on the Mount of Olives, his disciples came to him privately and said, "Tell us, when will these things happen? And what will be the sign of your coming and of the end of the age?" Jesus answered them, "Watch out that no one misleads you. For many will come in my name, saying, 'I am the Christ,' and they will mislead many. You will hear of wars and rumors of wars. Make sure that you are not alarmed, for this must happen, but the end is still to come. For nation will rise up in arms against nation, and kingdom against kingdom. And there will be famines and earthquakes in various places. All these things are the beginning of birth pains.

PERSECUTION OF DISCIPLES

"Then they will hand you over to be persecuted and will kill you. You will be hated by all the nations because of my name. Then many will be led into sin, and they will betray one another and hate one another. And many false prophets will appear and deceive many, and because lawlessness will increase so much, the love of many will grow cold. But the person who endures to the end will be saved. And this gospel of the kingdom will be preached throughout the whole inhabited earth as a testimony to all the nations, and then the end will come.

THE ABOMINATION OF DESOLATION

"So when you see *the abomination of desolation*—spoken about by Daniel the prophet—standing in the holy place" (let the reader understand), "then those in Judea must flee to the mountains. The one on the roof must not come down to take anything out of his house, and the one in the field must not turn back to get his cloak. Woe to those who are pregnant and to those who are nursing their babies in those days! Pray that your flight may not be in winter or on a Sabbath. For then there will be great suffering unlike anything that has happened from the beginning of the world until now, or ever will happen. And if those days had not been cut short, no one would be saved. But for the sake of the elect those days will be cut short. Then if anyone says to you, 'Look, here is the Christ!' or 'There he is!' do not believe him. For false messiahs and false prophets will appear and perform great signs and wonders to deceive, if possible, even the elect. Remember, I have told you ahead of time. So then, if someone says to you, 'Look, he is in the wilderness,' do not go out, or 'Look, he is in the inner rooms,' do not believe him. For just like the lightning comes from the east and flashes to the west, so the coming of the Son of Man will be. Wherever the corpse is, there the vultures will gather.

THE ARRIVAL OF THE SON OF MAN

"Immediately after the suffering of those days, *the sun will be darkened, and the moon will not give its light; the stars will fall from heaven, and the powers of heaven will be shaken.* Then the sign of the Son of Man will appear in heaven, and all the tribes of the earth will mourn. They will see *the Son of Man arriving on the clouds of heaven* with power and great glory. And he will send his angels with a loud trumpet blast, and they will gather his elect from the four winds, from one end of heaven to the other.

THE PARABLE OF THE FIG TREE

"Learn this parable from the fig tree: Whenever its branch becomes tender and puts out its leaves, you know that summer is near. So also you, when you see all these things, know that he is near, right at the door. I tell you the truth, this generation will not pass away until all these things take place. Heaven and earth will pass away, but my words will never pass away.

BE READY!

"But as for that day and hour no one knows it—not even the angels in heaven—except the Father alone. For just like the days of Noah were, so the coming of the Son of Man will be. For in those days before the flood, people were eating and drinking, marrying and giving in marriage, until the day Noah entered the ark. And they knew nothing until the flood came and took them all away. It will be the same at the coming of the Son of Man. Then there will be two men in the field; one will be taken and one left. There will be two women grinding grain with a mill; one will be taken and one left.

"Therefore stay alert because you do not know on what day your Lord will come. But understand this: If the owner of the house had known at what time of night the thief was coming, he would have been alert and would not have let his house be broken into. Therefore you also must be ready because the Son of Man will come at an hour when you do not expect him.

THE FAITHFUL AND WISE SLAVE

"Who then is the faithful and wise slave, whom the master has put in charge of his household, to give the other slaves their food at the proper time? Blessed is that slave whom the master finds at work when he comes. I tell you the truth, the master will put him in charge of all his possessions. But if that evil slave should say to himself, 'My master is staying away a long time,' and he begins to beat his fellow slaves and to eat and drink with drunkards, then the master of that slave will come on a day when he does not expect him and at an hour he does not foresee, and will cut him in two, and assign him a place with the hypocrites, where there will be weeping and gnashing of teeth.

CHAPTER 25

THE PARABLE OF THE 10 VIRGINS

"At that time the kingdom of heaven will be like 10 virgins who took their lamps and went out to meet the bridegroom. Five of the virgins were foolish, and five were wise. When the foolish ones took their lamps, they did not take extra olive oil with them. But the wise ones took flasks of olive oil with their lamps. When the bridegroom was delayed a long time, they all became drowsy and fell asleep. But at midnight there was a shout, 'Look, the bridegroom is here! Come out to meet him.' Then all the virgins woke up and trimmed their lamps. The foolish ones said to the wise, 'Give us some of your oil because our lamps are going out.' 'No,' they replied. 'There won't be enough for you and for us. Go instead to those who sell oil and buy some for yourselves.' But while they had gone to buy it, the bridegroom arrived, and those who were ready went inside with him to the wedding banquet. Then the door was shut. Later, the other virgins came too, saying, 'Lord, lord! Let us in!' But he replied, 'I tell you the truth, I do not know you!' Therefore stay alert because you do not know the day or the hour.

THE PARABLE OF THE TALENTS

"For it is like a man going on a journey, who summoned his slaves and entrusted his property to them. To one he gave five talents, to another two, and to another one, each according to his ability. Then he went on his journey. The one who had received five talents went off right away and put his money to work and gained five more. In the same way, the one who had two gained two more. But the one who had received one talent went out and dug a hole in the ground and hid his master's money in it. After a long time, the master of those slaves came and settled his accounts with them. The one who had received the five talents came and brought five more, saying, 'Sir, you entrusted me with five talents. See, I have gained five more.' His master answered, 'Well done, good and faithful slave! You have been faithful in a few things. I will put you in charge of many things. Enter into the joy of your master.' The one with the two talents also came and said, 'Sir, you entrusted two talents to me. See, I have gained two more.' His master answered, 'Well done, good and faithful slave! You have been faithful with a few things. I will put you in charge of many things. Enter into the joy of your master.' Then the one who had received the one talent came and said, 'Sir, I knew that you were a hard man, harvesting where you did not sow, and gathering where you did not scatter seed, so I was afraid, and I went and hid your talent in the ground. See, you have what is yours.' But his master answered, 'Evil and lazy slave! So you knew that I harvest where I didn't sow and gather where I didn't scatter? Then you should have deposited my money with the bankers, and on my return I would have received my money back with interest! Therefore take the talent from him and give it to the one who has 10. For the one who has will be given more, and he will have more than enough. But the one who does not have, even what he has will be taken from him. And throw that worthless slave into the outer darkness, where there will be weeping and gnashing of teeth.'

THE JUDGMENT

"When the Son of Man comes in his glory and all the angels with him, then he will sit on his glorious throne. All the nations will be assembled before him, and he will separate people one from another like a shepherd separates the sheep from the goats. He will put the sheep on his right and the goats on his left. Then the king will say to those on his right, 'Come, you who are blessed by my Father, inherit the kingdom prepared for you from the foundation of the world. For I was hungry and you gave me food, I was thirsty and you gave me something to drink, I was a stranger and you invited me in, I was naked and you gave me clothing, I was sick and you took care of me, I was in prison and you visited me.' Then the righteous will answer him, 'Lord, when did we see you hungry and feed you, or thirsty and give you something to drink? When did we see you a stranger and invite you in, or naked and clothe you? When did we see you sick or in prison and visit you?' And the king will answer them, 'I tell you the truth, just as you did it for one of the least of these brothers or sisters of mine, you did it for me.'

"Then he will say to those on his left, 'Depart from me, you accursed, into the eternal fire that has been prepared for the devil and his angels! For I was hungry and you gave me nothing to eat, I was thirsty and you gave me nothing to drink. I was a stranger and you did not receive me as a guest, naked and you did not clothe me, sick and in prison and you did not visit me.' Then they too will answer, 'Lord, when did we see you hungry or thirsty or a stranger or naked or sick or in prison, and did not give you whatever you needed?' Then he will answer them, 'I tell you the truth, just as you did not do it for one of the least of these, you did not do it for me.' And these will depart into eternal punishment, but the righteous into eternal life."

CHAPTER 26

THE PLOT AGAINST JESUS

When Jesus had finished saying all these things, he told his disciples, "You know that after two days the Passover is coming, and the Son of Man will be handed over to be crucified." Then the chief priests and the elders of the people met together in the palace of the high priest, who was named Caiaphas. They planned to arrest Jesus by stealth and kill him. But they said, "Not during the feast, so that there won't be a riot among the people."

JESUS' ANOINTING

Now while Jesus was in Bethany at the house of Simon the leper, a woman came to him with an alabaster jar of expensive perfumed oil, and she poured it on his head as he was at the table. When the disciples saw this, they became indignant and said, "Why this waste? It could have been sold at a high price and the money given to the poor!" When Jesus learned of this, he said to them, "Why are you bothering this woman? She has done a good service for me. For you will always have the poor with you, but you will not always have me! When she poured this oil on my body, she did it to prepare me for burial. I tell you the truth, wherever this gospel is proclaimed in the whole world, what she has done will also be told in memory of her."

THE PLAN TO BETRAY JESUS

Then one of the twelve, the one named Judas Iscariot, went to the chief priests and said, "What will you give me to betray him into your hands?" So they set out 30 silver coins for him. From that time on, Judas began looking for an opportunity to betray him.

THE PASSOVER

Now on the first day of the Feast of Unleavened Bread the disciples came to Jesus and said, "Where do you want us to prepare for you to eat the Passover?" He said, "Go into the city to a certain man and tell him, 'The Teacher says, "My time is near. I will observe the Passover with my disciples at your house."'" So the disciples did as Jesus had instructed them, and they prepared the Passover. When it was evening, he took his place at the table with the twelve. And while they were eating he said, "I tell you the truth, one of you will betray me." They became greatly distressed and each one began to say to him, "Surely not I, Lord?" He answered, "The one who has dipped his hand into the bowl with me will betray me. The Son of Man will go as it is written about him, but woe to that man by whom the Son of Man is betrayed! It would be better for him if he had never been born." Then Judas, the one who would betray him, said, "Surely not I, Rabbi?" Jesus replied, "You have said it yourself."

THE LORD'S SUPPER

While they were eating, Jesus took bread, and after giving thanks he broke it, gave it to his disciples, and said, "Take, eat, this is my body." And after taking the cup and giving thanks, he gave it to them, saying, "Drink from it, all of you, for this is my blood, the blood of the covenant, that is poured out for many for the forgiveness of sins. I tell you, from now on I will not drink of this fruit of the vine until that day when I drink it new with you in my Father's kingdom." After singing a hymn, they went out to the Mount of Olives.

THE PREDICTION OF PETER'S DENIAL

Then Jesus said to them, "This night you will all fall away because of me, for it is written:

> *'I will strike the shepherd,*
> *and the sheep of the flock will be*
> *scattered.'*

But after I am raised, I will go ahead of you into Galilee." Peter said to him, "If they all fall away because of you, I will never fall away!" Jesus said to him, "I tell you the truth, on this night, before the rooster crows, you will deny me three times." Peter said to him, "Even if I must die with you, I will never deny you." And all the disciples said the same thing.

GETHSEMANE

Then Jesus went with them to a place called Gethsemane, and he said to the disciples, "Sit here while I go over there and pray." He took with him Peter and the two sons of Zebedee, and he became anguished and distressed. Then he said to them, "My soul is deeply grieved, even to the point of death. Remain here and stay awake with me." Going a little farther, he threw himself down with his face to the ground and prayed, "My Father, if possible, let this cup pass from me! Yet not what I will, but what you will." Then he came to the disciples and found them sleeping. He said to Peter, "So, couldn't you stay awake with me for one hour? Stay awake and pray that you will not fall into temptation. The spirit is willing, but the flesh is weak." He went away a second time and prayed, "My Father, if this cup cannot be taken away unless I drink it, your will must be done." He came again and found them sleeping; they could not keep their eyes open. So leaving them again, he went away and prayed for the third time, saying the same thing once more. Then he came to the disciples and said to them, "Are you still sleeping and resting? Look, the hour is approaching, and the Son of Man is betrayed into the hands of sinners. Get up, let us go. Look! My betrayer is approaching!"

BETRAYAL AND ARREST

While he was still speaking, Judas, one of the twelve, arrived. With him was a large crowd armed with swords and clubs, sent by the chief priests and elders of the people. (Now the betrayer had given them a sign, saying, "The one I kiss is the man. Arrest him!") Immediately he went up to Jesus and said, "Greetings, Rabbi," and kissed him. Jesus said to him, "Friend, do what you are here to do." Then they came and took hold of Jesus and arrested him. But one of those with Jesus grabbed his sword, drew it out, and struck the high priest's slave, cutting off his ear. Then Jesus said to him, "Put your sword back in its place! For all who take hold of the sword will die by the sword. Or do you think that I cannot call on my Father and that he would send me more than 12 legions of angels right now? How then would the scriptures that say it must happen this way be fulfilled?" At that moment Jesus said to the crowd, "Have you come out with swords and clubs to arrest me like you would an outlaw? Day after day I sat teaching in the temple courts, yet you did not arrest me. But this has happened so that the scriptures of the prophets would be fulfilled." Then all the disciples left him and fled.

CONDEMNED BY THE SANHEDRIN

Now the ones who had arrested Jesus led him to Caiaphas, the high priest, in whose house the experts in the law and the elders had gathered. But Peter was following him from a distance, all the way to the high priest's courtyard. After going in, he sat with the guards to see the outcome. The chief priests and the whole Sanhedrin were trying to find false testimony against Jesus so that they could put him to death. But they did not find anything, though many false witnesses came forward. Finally two came forward and declared, "This man said, 'I am able to destroy the temple of God and rebuild it in three days.'" So the high priest stood up and said to him, "Have you no answer? What is this that they are testifying against you?" But Jesus was silent. The high priest said to him, "I charge you under oath by the living God, tell us if you are the Christ, the Son of God." Jesus said to him, "You have said it yourself. But I tell you, from now on you will see the Son of Man *sitting at the right hand* of the Power and *coming on the clouds of heaven.*" Then the high priest tore his clothes and declared, "He has blasphemed! Why do we still need witnesses? Now you have heard the blasphemy! What is your verdict?" They answered, "He is guilty and deserves death." Then they spat in his face and struck him with their fists. And some slapped him, saying, "Prophesy for us, you Christ! Who hit you?"

PETER'S DENIALS

Now Peter was sitting outside in the courtyard. A slave girl came to him and said, "You also were with Jesus the Galilean." But he denied it in front of them all: "I don't know what you're talking about!" When he went out to the gateway, another slave girl saw him and said to the people there, "This man was with Jesus the Nazarene." He denied it again with an oath, "I do not know the man!" After a little while, those standing there came up to Peter and said, "You really are one of them too—even your accent gives you away!" At that he began to curse, and he swore with an oath, "I do not know the man!" At that moment a rooster crowed. Then Peter remembered what Jesus had said: "Before the rooster crows, you will deny me three times." And he went outside and wept bitterly.

CHAPTER 27

JESUS BROUGHT BEFORE PILATE

When it was early in the morning, all the chief priests and the elders of the people plotted against Jesus to execute him. They tied him up, led him away, and handed him over to Pilate the governor.

JUDAS' SUICIDE

Now when Judas, who had betrayed him, saw that Jesus had been condemned, he regretted what he had done and returned the

30 silver coins to the chief priests and the elders, saying, "I have sinned by betraying innocent blood!" But they said, "What is that to us? You take care of it yourself!" So Judas threw the silver coins into the temple and left. Then he went out and hanged himself. The chief priests took the silver and said, "It is not lawful to put this into the temple treasury, since it is blood money." After consulting together they bought the Potter's Field with it, as a burial place for foreigners. For this reason that field has been called the "Field of Blood" to this day. Then what was spoken by Jeremiah the prophet was fulfilled: *They took the 30 silver coins, the price of the one whose price had been set by the people of Israel, and they gave them for the potter's field, as the Lord commanded me.*

JESUS AND PILATE

Then Jesus stood before the governor, and the governor asked him, "Are you the king of the Jews?" Jesus said, "You say so." But when he was accused by the chief priests and the elders, he did not respond. Then Pilate said to him, "Don't you hear how many charges they are bringing against you?" But he did not answer even one accusation, so that the governor was quite amazed.

During the feast the governor was accustomed to release one prisoner to the crowd, whomever they wanted. At that time they had

in custody a notorious prisoner named Jesus
Barabbas. So after they had assembled, Pilate
said to them, "Whom do you want me to release for you, Jesus Barabbas or Jesus who is
called the Christ?" (For he knew that they had
handed him over because of envy.) As he was
sitting on the judgment seat, his wife sent a
message to him: "Have nothing to do with that
innocent man; I have suffered greatly as a result of a dream about him today." But the chief
priests and the elders persuaded the crowds
to ask for Barabbas and to have Jesus killed.
The governor asked them, "Which of the two
do you want me to release for you?" And they
said, "Barabbas!" Pilate said to them, "Then
what should I do with Jesus who is called the
Christ?" They all said, "Crucify him!" He asked,
"Why? What wrong has he done?" But they
shouted more insistently, "Crucify him!"

JESUS IS CONDEMNED AND MOCKED

When Pilate saw that he could do nothing,
but that instead a riot was starting, he took
some water, washed his hands before the
crowd and said, "I am innocent of this man's
blood. You take care of it yourselves!" In re-
ply all the people said, "Let his blood be on us
and on our children!" Then he released Barabbas for them. But after he had Jesus flogged,
he handed him over to be crucified. Then the
governor's soldiers took Jesus into the governor's residence and gathered the whole cohort

around him. They stripped him and put a scarlet robe around him, and after braiding a crown of thorns, they put it on his head. They put a staff in his right hand, and kneeling down before him, they mocked him: "Hail, king of the Jews!" They spat on him and took the staff and struck him repeatedly on the head. When they had mocked him, they stripped him of the robe and put his own clothes back on him. Then they led him away to crucify him.

THE CRUCIFIXION

As they were going out, they found a man from Cyrene named Simon, whom they forced to carry his cross. They came to a place called Golgotha (which means "Place of the Skull") and offered Jesus wine mixed with gall to drink. But after tasting it, he would not drink it. When they had crucified him, *they divided his clothes by throwing dice.* Then they sat down and kept guard over him there. Above his head they put the charge against him, which read: "This is Jesus, the king of the Jews." Then two outlaws were crucified with him, one on his right and one on his left. Those who passed by defamed him, shaking their heads and saying, "You who can destroy the temple and rebuild it in three days, save yourself! If you are God's Son, come down from the cross!" In the same way even the chief priests—together with the experts in the law and elders—were mocking him: "He saved others, but he cannot save himself! He is the king of Israel! If he comes down now from the cross, we will believe in him! *He trusts in God—let God, if he wants to, deliver him now* because he said, 'I am God's Son'!" The robbers who were crucified with him also spoke abusively to him.

JESUS' DEATH

Now from noon until three, darkness came over all the land. At about three o'clock Jesus shouted with a loud voice, *"Eli, Eli, lema sabachthani?"* that is, ***"My God, my God, why have you forsaken me?"*** When some of the bystanders heard it, they said, "This man is calling for Elijah." Immediately one of them ran and got a sponge, filled it with sour wine, put it on a stick, and gave it to him to drink. But the rest said, "Leave him alone! Let's see if Elijah will come to save him." Then Jesus cried out again with a loud voice and gave up his spirit. Just then the temple curtain was torn in two, from top to bottom. The earth shook and the rocks were split apart. And tombs were opened, and the bodies of many saints who had died were raised. (They came out of the tombs after his resurrection and went into the holy city and appeared to many people.) Now when the centurion and those with him who were guarding Jesus saw the earthquake and what took place, they were extremely terrified and said, "Truly this one was God's Son!" Many women who had followed Jesus from Galilee and given him support were also there, watching from a distance. Among them were Mary Magdalene, Mary the mother of James and Joseph, and the mother of the sons of Zebedee.

JESUS' BURIAL

Now when it was evening, there came a rich man from Arimathea, named Joseph, who was also a disciple of Jesus. He went to Pilate and asked for the body of Jesus. Then Pilate ordered that it be given to him. Joseph took the body, wrapped it in a clean linen cloth, and placed it in his own new tomb that he had cut in the rock. Then he rolled a great stone across the entrance of the tomb and went away. (Now Mary Magdalene and the other Mary were sitting there, opposite the tomb.)

THE GUARD AT THE TOMB

The next day (which is after the day of preparation) the chief priests and the Pharisees assembled before Pilate and said, "Sir, we remember that while that deceiver was still alive he said, 'After three days I will rise again.' So give orders to secure the tomb until the third day. Otherwise his disciples may come and steal his body and say to the people, 'He has been raised from the dead,' and the last deception will be worse than the first." Pilate said to them, "Take a guard of soldiers. Go and make it as secure as you can." So they went with the soldiers of the guard and made the tomb secure by sealing the stone.

CHAPTER 28

THE RESURRECTION

Now after the Sabbath, at dawn on the first day of the week, Mary Magdalene and the other Mary went to look at the tomb. Suddenly there was a severe earthquake, for an angel of the Lord descending from heaven came and rolled away the stone and sat on it. His appearance was like lightning, and his clothes were white as snow. The guards were shaken and became like dead men because they were so afraid of him. But the angel said to the women, "Do not be afraid; I know that you are looking for Jesus, who was crucified. He is not here, for he has been raised, just as he said. Come and see the place where he was lying. Then go quickly and tell his disciples, 'He has been raised from the dead. He is going ahead of you into Galilee. You will see him there.' Listen, I have told you!" So they left the tomb quickly, with fear and great joy, and ran to tell his disciples. But Jesus met them, saying, "Greetings!" They came to him, held on to his feet and worshiped him. Then Jesus said to them, "Do not be afraid. Go and tell my brothers to go to Galilee. They will see me there."

THE GUARDS' REPORT

While they were going, some of the guards went into the city and told the chief priests everything that had happened. After they had assembled with the elders and formed a plan, they gave a large sum of money to the soldiers, telling them, "You are to say, 'His disciples came at night and stole his body while we were asleep.' If this matter is heard before the governor, we will satisfy him and keep you out of trouble." So they took the money and did as they were instructed. And this story is told among the Jews to this day.

THE GREAT COMMISSION

So the 11 disciples went to Galilee to the mountain Jesus had designated. When they saw him, they worshiped him, but some doubted. Then Jesus came up and said to them, "All authority in heaven and on earth has been given to me. Therefore go and make disciples of all nations, baptizing them in the name of the Father and the Son and the Holy Spirit, teaching them to obey everything I have commanded you. And remember, I am with you always, to the end of the age."

HEBREWS

PROLOGUE

Jesus' life was marked by persecution. Even though he did no wrong, just a few of his people accepted him. Should his followers expect anything less? Jesus had even warned them that anyone who followed him would face hardship.

It didn't take long for Jesus' warning to prove true. As the early Christians began declaring that Jesus is the Messiah, their fellow Jews responded in anger. Jesus couldn't be the Messiah. He hadn't delivered them from anything. He hadn't led an uprising against the Roman forces occupying their homeland. He hadn't even tried. He couldn't even save himself from being executed as a criminal on a Roman cross. And now his followers wanted everyone to worship him as God? That was not just foolishness, it was blasphemy. If there was one lesson that the Jews had learned during their history, it was the danger of worshiping more than one God. They weren't about to repeat that mistake with Jesus.

The response was quick and severe. The Christians were rejected by their families.

They were banned in the marketplace. Hostility followed them wherever they went. It was too much for some to bear. They began to wonder if they should return to Judaism.

Amid this confusion and wavering, a leader in the church wrote this letter to encourage them. They couldn't give up. They couldn't leave Christianity and return to Judaism. And he gave them a compelling reason why.

CHAPTER 1

INTRODUCTION: GOD HAS SPOKEN FULLY AND FINALLY IN HIS SON

After God spoke long ago in various portions and in various ways to our ancestors through the prophets, in these last days he has spoken to us in a son, whom he appointed heir of all things, and through whom he created the world. The Son is the radiance of his glory and the representation of his essence, and he sustains all things by his powerful word, and so when he had accomplished cleansing for sins, *he sat down at the right hand of the Majesty on high.* Thus he became so far better than the angels as he has inherited a name superior to theirs.

THE SON IS SUPERIOR TO ANGELS

For to which of the angels did God ever say, *"You are my son! Today I have fathered you"*?

And in another place he says, *"I will be his father and he will be my son."* But when he again brings his firstborn into the world, he says, *"Let all the angels of God worship him!"* And he says of the angels, *"He makes his angels winds and his ministers a flame of fire,"* but of the Son he says,

> *"Your throne, O God, is forever and ever,*
> *and a righteous scepter is the scepter of*
> *your kingdom.*
> *You have loved righteousness and hated*
> *lawlessness.*
> *So God, your God, has anointed you*
> *over your companions with the oil of*
> *rejoicing."*

And,

> *"You founded the earth in the beginning,*
> *Lord,*
> *and the heavens are the works of your hands.*
> *They will perish, but you continue.*
> *And they will all grow old like a garment,*
> *and like a robe you will fold them up*
> *and* like a garment *they will be changed,*
> *but you are the same and your years will*
> *never run out."*

But to which of the angels has he ever said, *"Sit at my right hand until I make your enemies a footstool for your feet"*? Are they not all ministering spirits, sent out to serve those who will inherit salvation?

CHAPTER 2

WARNING AGAINST DRIFTING AWAY

Therefore we must pay closer attention to what we have heard, so that we do not drift away. For if the message spoken through angels proved to be so firm that every violation or disobedience received its just penalty, how will we escape if we neglect such a great salvation? It was first communicated through the Lord and was confirmed to us by those who heard him, while God confirmed their witness with signs and wonders and various miracles and gifts of the Holy Spirit distributed according to his will.

EXPOSITION OF PSALM 8: JESUS AND THE DESTINY OF HUMANITY

For he did not put the world to come, about which we are speaking, under the control of angels. Instead someone testified somewhere:

"What is man that you think of him or the son of man that you care for him?
You made him lower than the angels for a little while.
You crowned him with glory and honor.
You put all things under his control."

For when he *put all things under his control,* he left nothing outside of his control. At present we do not yet see *all things under his control,* but we see Jesus, who was made *lower than the angels for a little while,* now crowned with glory and honor because he suffered death, so that by God's grace he would experience death on behalf of everyone. For it was fitting for him, for whom and through whom all things exist, in bringing many sons to glory, to make the pioneer of their salvation perfect through sufferings. For indeed he who makes holy and those being made holy all have the same origin, and so he is not ashamed to call them brothers and sisters, saying, *"I will proclaim your name to my brothers; in the midst of the assembly I will praise you."* Again he says, "I will be confident in him," and again, *"Here I am, with the children God has given me."* Therefore, since the children share in flesh and blood, he likewise shared in their humanity, so that through death he could destroy the one who holds the power of death (that is, the devil), and set free those who were held in slavery all their lives by their fear of death. For surely his concern is not for angels, but he is concerned for Abraham's descendants. Therefore he had to be made like his brothers and sisters in every respect, so that he could become a merciful and faithful high priest in things relating to God, to make atonement for the sins of the people. For since he himself suffered when he was tempted, he is able to help those who are tempted.

CHAPTER 3

JESUS AND MOSES

Therefore, holy brothers and sisters, partners in a heavenly calling, take note of Jesus, the apostle and high priest whom we confess, who is faithful to the one who appointed him, as Moses was also in God's house. For he has come to deserve greater glory than Moses, just as the builder of a house deserves greater honor than the house itself! For every house is built by someone, but the builder of all things is God. Now Moses was *faithful in all God's house* as a servant, to testify to the things that would be spoken. But Christ is faithful as a son over God's house. We are of his house, if in fact we hold firmly to our confidence and the hope we take pride in.

EXPOSITION OF PSALM 95: HEARING GOD'S WORD IN FAITH

Therefore, as the Holy Spirit says,
"Oh, that today you would listen as he speaks!
Do not harden your hearts as in the
rebellion, in the day of testing in the
wilderness.
There your fathers tested me and tried me,
and they saw my works for forty years.
Therefore, I became provoked at that
generation and said, 'Their hearts are
always wandering, and they have not
known my ways.'
As I swore in my anger, 'They will never
enter my rest!'"

See to it, brothers and sisters, that none of you has an evil, unbelieving heart that forsakes the living God. But exhort one another each day, as long as it is called "Today," that none of you may become hardened by sin's deception. For we have become partners with Christ, if in fact we hold our initial confidence firm until the end. As it says, *"Oh, that today you would listen as he speaks! Do not harden your hearts as in the rebellion."* For which ones heard and rebelled? Was it not all who came out of Egypt under Moses' leadership? And against whom was God provoked for forty years? Was it not those who sinned, *whose dead bodies fell in the wilderness?* And to whom did he swear they would never enter into his rest, except those who were disobedient? So we see that they could not enter because of unbelief.

CHAPTER 4

GOD'S PROMISED REST

Therefore we must be wary that, while the promise of entering his rest remains open, none of you may seem to have come short of it. For we had good news proclaimed to us just as they did. But the message they heard did them no good, since they did not join in with those who heard it in faith. For we who have believed enter that rest, as he has said, *"As I swore in my anger, 'They will never enter my rest!'"* And yet God's works were accomplished from the foundation of the world. For he has spoken somewhere about the seventh day in this way: "*And God rested on the seventh day from all his works*," but to repeat the text cited earlier: "*They will never enter my rest!*" Therefore it remains for some to enter it, yet those to whom it was previously proclaimed did not enter because of disobedience. So God again ordains a certain day, "Today," speaking through David after so long a time, as in the words quoted before, "*Oh, that today you would listen as he speaks! Do not harden your hearts.*" For if Joshua had given them rest, God would not have spoken afterward about another day. Consequently a Sabbath rest remains for the people of God. For the one who enters God's rest has also rested from his works, just as God did from his own works. Thus we must make every effort to enter that rest, so that no one may fall by following the same pattern of disobedience. For the word of God is living and active and sharper than any double-edged sword, piercing even to the point of dividing soul from spirit, and joints from marrow; it is able to judge the desires and thoughts of the heart. And no creature is hidden from God, but everything is naked and exposed to the eyes of him to whom we must render an account.

JESUS OUR COMPASSIONATE HIGH PRIEST

Therefore since we have a great high priest who has passed through the heavens, Jesus the Son of God, let us hold fast to our confession.

For we do not have a high priest incapable of sympathizing with our weaknesses, but one who has been tempted in every way just as we are, yet without sin. Therefore let us confidently approach the throne of grace to receive mercy and find grace whenever we need help.

CHAPTER 5

For every high priest is taken from among the people and appointed to represent them before God, to offer both gifts and sacrifices for sins. He is able to deal compassionately with those who are ignorant and erring, since he also is subject to weakness, and for this reason he is obligated to make sin offerings for himself as well as for the people. And no one assumes this honor on his own initiative, but only when called to it by God, as in fact Aaron was. So also Christ did not glorify himself in becoming high priest, but the one who glorified him was God, who said to him, *"You are my Son! Today I have fathered you,"* as also in another place God says, *"You are a priest forever in the order of Melchizedek."* During his earthly life Christ offered both requests and supplications, with loud cries and tears, to the one who was able to save him from death, and he was heard because of his devotion. Although he was a son, he learned obedience through the things he suffered. And by being perfected in this way, he became the source of eternal salvation to all who obey him, and he was designated by God as high priest *in the order of Melchizedek.*

THE NEED TO MOVE ON TO MATURITY

On this topic we have much to say, and it is difficult to explain, since you have become sluggish in hearing. For though you should in fact be teachers by this time, you need someone to teach you the beginning elements of God's utterances. You have gone back to needing milk, not solid food. For everyone who lives on milk is inexperienced in the message of righteousness because he is an infant. But solid food is for the mature, whose perceptions are trained by practice to discern both good and evil.

CHAPTER 6

Therefore we must progress beyond the elementary instructions about Christ and move on to maturity, not laying this foundation again: repentance from dead works and faith in God, teaching about ritual washings, laying on of hands, resurrection of the dead, and eternal judgment. And this is what we intend to do, if God permits. For it is impossible in the case of those who have once been enlightened, tasted the heavenly gift, become partakers of the Holy Spirit, tasted the good word of God and the miracles of the coming age, and then have committed apostasy, to renew them again to repentance, since they are crucifying the Son of God for themselves all over again and holding him up to contempt. For the ground that has soaked up the rain that frequently falls on it and yields useful vegetation for those who tend it receives a blessing from God. But if it produces thorns and thistles, it is useless and about to be cursed; its fate is to be burned. But in your case, dear friends, even though we speak like this, we are convinced of better things relating to salvation. For God is not unjust so as to forget your work and the love you have demonstrated for his name, in having served and continuing to serve the saints. But we passionately want each of you to demonstrate the same eagerness for the fulfillment of your hope until the end, so that you may not be sluggish, but imitators of those who through faith and perseverance inherit the promises.

Now when God made his promise to Abraham, since he could swear by no one greater, he swore by himself, saying, "*Surely I will bless you greatly and multiply your descendants abundantly.*" And so by persevering, Abraham inherited the promise. For people swear by something greater than themselves, and the oath serves as a confirmation to end all dispute. In the same way God wanted to demonstrate more clearly to the heirs of the promise that his purpose was unchangeable, and so he intervened with an oath, so that we who have found refuge in him may find strong encouragement to hold fast to the hope set before us through two unchangeable things, since it is impossible for God to lie. We have this hope as an anchor for the soul, sure and steadfast, which reaches inside behind the curtain, where Jesus our forerunner entered on our behalf, since he became *a priest forever in the order of Melchizedek.*

CHAPTER 7

THE NATURE OF MELCHIZEDEK'S PRIESTHOOD

Now this *Melchizedek, king of Salem, priest of the most high God, met Abraham as he was returning from defeating the kings* and *blessed him.* To him also *Abraham apportioned a tithe of everything.* His name first means king of righteousness, then *king of Salem,* that is, king of peace. Without father, without mother, without genealogy, he has neither beginning of days nor end of life but is like the son of God, and he remains a priest for all time. But see how great he must be, if Abraham the patriarch gave him a tithe of his plunder. And those of the sons of Levi who receive the priestly office have authorization according to the law to collect a tithe from the people, that is, from their fellow countrymen, although they, too, are descendants of Abraham. But Melchizedek who does not share their ancestry collected a tithe from Abraham and blessed the one who possessed the promise. Now without dispute the inferior is blessed by the superior, and in one case tithes are received by mortal men, while in the other by him who is affirmed to be alive. And it could be said that Levi himself, who receives tithes, paid a tithe through Abraham. For he was still in his ancestor Abraham's loins when Melchizedek met him.

JESUS AND THE PRIESTHOOD OF MELCHIZEDEK

So if perfection had in fact been possible through the Levitical priesthood—for on that basis the people received the law—what further need would there have been for another priest to arise, said to be in the order of Melchizedek and not in Aaron's order? For when the priesthood changes, a change in the law must come as well. Yet the one these things are spoken about belongs to a different tribe, and no one from that tribe has ever officiated at the altar. For it is clear that our Lord is descended from Judah, yet Moses said nothing about priests in connection with that tribe. And this is even clearer if another priest arises in the likeness of Melchizedek, who has become a priest not by a legal regulation about physical descent but by the power of an indestructible life. For here is the testimony about him: *"You are a priest forever in the order of Melchizedek."* On the one hand a former command is set aside because it is weak and useless, for the law made nothing perfect. On the other hand a better hope is introduced, through which we draw near to God. And since this was not done without a sworn affirmation—for the others have become priests without a sworn affirmation, but Jesus did so with a sworn affirmation by the one who said to him, *"The Lord has sworn and will not change his mind, 'You are a priest forever'* "—accordingly Jesus has become the guarantee of a better covenant. And the others who became priests were numerous because death prevented them from continuing in office, but he holds his priesthood permanently since he lives forever. So he is able to save completely those who come to God through him because he always lives to intercede for them. For it is indeed fitting for us to have such a high priest: holy, innocent, undefiled, separate from sinners, and exalted above the heavens. He has no need to do every day what those priests do, to offer sacrifices first for their own sins and then for the sins of the people, since he did this in offering himself once for all. For the law appoints as high priests men subject to weakness, but the word of solemn affirmation that came after the law appoints a son made perfect forever.

CHAPTER 8

THE HIGH PRIEST OF A BETTER COVENANT

Now the main point of what we are saying is this: We have such a high priest, one who *sat down at the right hand of the throne of the Maj-esty in heaven,* a minister in the sanctuary and the true tabernacle that the Lord, not man, set up. For every high priest is appointed to offer both gifts and sacrifices. So this one, too, had to have something to offer. Now if he were on earth, he would not be a priest, since there are already priests who offer the gifts prescribed by the law. The place where they serve is a sketch and shadow of the heavenly sanctuary, just as Moses was warned by God as he was about to complete the tabernacle. For he says, **"See that you make everything according to the design shown to you on the mountain."** But now Jesus has obtained a superior ministry, since the covenant that he mediates is also better and is enacted on better promises.

For if that first covenant had been faultless, no one would have looked for a second one. But showing its fault, God says to them,

> **"Look, the days are coming, says the Lord,
> when I will complete a new covenant
> with the house of Israel and with the
> house of Judah.
> It will not be like the covenant that I made
> with their fathers, on the day when I
> took them by the hand to lead them out
> of Egypt, because they did not continue
> in my covenant, and I had no regard for
> them, says the Lord.**

*For this is the covenant that I will establish
with the house of Israel after those days,
says the Lord. I will put my laws in their
minds, and I will inscribe them on their
hearts. And I will be their God, and they
will be my people.*

*And there will be no need at all for each
one to teach his countryman or each one
to teach his brother saying, 'Know the
Lord,' since they will all know me, from
the least to the greatest.*

*For I will be merciful toward their evil
deeds, and their sins I will remember no
longer."*

When he speaks of a new covenant, he
makes the first obsolete. Now what is grow-
ing obsolete and aging is about to disappear.

CHAPTER 9

THE ARRANGEMENT AND RITUAL
OF THE EARTHLY SANCTUARY

Now the first covenant, in fact, had regulations for worship and its earthly sanctuary. For a tent was prepared, the outer one,
which contained the lampstand, the table, and the presentation of the loaves; this
is called the Holy Place. And after the second curtain there was a tent called the holy
of holies. It contained the golden altar of in-
cense and the ark of the covenant covered en-
tirely with gold. In this ark were the golden

urn containing the manna, Aaron's rod that budded, and the stone tablets of the covenant. And above the ark were the cherubim of glory overshadowing the mercy seat. Now is not the time to speak of these things in detail. So with these things prepared like this, the priests enter continually into the outer tent as they perform their duties. But only the high priest enters once a year into the inner tent, and not without blood that he offers for himself and for the sins of the people committed in ignorance. The Holy Spirit is making clear that the way into the Holy Place had not yet appeared as long as the old tabernacle was standing. This was a symbol for the time then present, when gifts and sacrifices were offered that could not perfect the conscience of the worshiper. They served only for matters of food and drink and various ritual washings; they are external regulations imposed until the new order came.

CHRIST'S SERVICE IN THE HEAVENLY SANCTUARY

But now Christ has come as the high priest of the good things to come. He passed through the greater and more perfect tent not made with hands, that is, not of this creation, and he entered once for all into the Most Holy Place not by the blood of goats and calves but by his own blood, and so he himself secured eternal redemption. For if the blood of goats and bulls and the ashes of a young cow sprinkled on those who are defiled consecrated them and provided ritual purity, how much more will the blood of Christ, who through the eternal Spirit offered himself without blemish to God, purify our consciences from dead works to worship the living God.

And so he is the mediator of a new covenant, so that those who are called may receive the eternal inheritance he has promised, since he died to set them free from the violations committed under the first covenant. For where there is a will, the death of the one who made it must be proven. For a will takes effect only at death, since it carries no force while the one who made it is alive. So even the first covenant was inaugurated with blood. For when Moses had spoken every command to all the people according to the law, he took the blood of calves and goats with water and scarlet wool and hyssop and sprinkled both the book itself and all the people, and said, *"This is the blood of the covenant that God has commanded you to keep."* And both the tabernacle and all the utensils of worship he likewise sprinkled with blood. Indeed according to the law almost everything was purified with blood, and without the shedding of blood there is no forgiveness. So it was necessary for the sketches of the things in heaven to be purified with these sacrifices, but the heavenly things themselves required better sacrifices than these. For Christ did not enter a sanctuary made with hands—the representation of the true sanctuary—but into heaven itself, and he appears now in God's presence for us. And he did not enter to offer himself again and again, the way the high priest enters the sanctuary year after year with blood that is not his own, for then he would have had to suffer again and again since the foundation of the world. But now he has appeared once for all at the consummation of the ages to put away sin by his sacrifice. And just as people are appointed to die once, and then to face judgment, so also, after Christ was offered once to *bear the sins of many,* to those who eagerly await him he will appear a second time, not to bear sin but to bring salvation.

CHAPTER 10

CONCLUDING EXPOSITION: OLD AND NEW SACRIFICES CONTRASTED

For the law possesses a shadow of the good things to come but not the reality itself, and is therefore completely unable, by the same sacrifices offered continually, year after year, to perfect those who come to worship. For otherwise would they not have ceased to be offered, since the worshipers would have been purified once for all and so have no further consciousness of sin? But in those sacrifices there is a reminder of sins year after year. For it is impossible for the blood of bulls and goats to take away sins. So when he came into the world, he said,

> *"Sacrifice and offering you did not desire,*
>   *but a body you prepared for me.*
> *Whole burnt offerings and sin-offerings*
>   *you took no delight in.*
> *Then I said, 'Here I am: I have come—it*
>   *is written of me in the scroll of the*
>   *book—to do your will, O God.'"*

When he says above, *"Sacrifices and offerings* and *whole burnt offerings and sin-offerings you did not desire nor did you take delight* in them" (which are offered according to the law), then he says, *"Here I am: I have come to do your will."* He does away with the first to establish the second. By his will we have been made holy through the offering of the body of Jesus Christ once for all. And every priest stands day after day serving and offering the same sacrifices again and again—sacrifices that can never take away sins. But when this priest had offered one sacrifice for sins for all time, *he sat down at the right hand* of God, where he is now waiting *until his enemies are made a footstool for his feet.* For by one offering he has perfected for all time those who are made holy. And the Holy Spirit also witnesses to us, for after saying, *"This is the covenant that I will establish with them after those days, says the Lord. I will put my laws on their hearts and I will inscribe them on their minds,"* then he says, *"Their sins and their lawless deeds I will remember no longer."* Now where there is forgiveness of these, there is no longer any offering for sin.

DRAWING NEAR TO GOD IN ENDURING FAITH

Therefore, brothers and sisters, since we have confidence to enter the sanctuary by the blood of Jesus, by the fresh and living way that he inaugurated for us through the curtain, that is, through his flesh, and since we have a great priest over the house of God, let us draw near with a sincere heart in the assurance that faith brings, because we have had our hearts sprinkled clean from an evil conscience and our bodies washed in pure water. And let us hold unwaveringly to the hope that we confess, for the one who made the promise is trustworthy. And let us take thought of how to spur one another on to love and good works, not abandoning our own meetings, as some are in the habit of doing, but encouraging each other, and even more so because you see the day drawing near.

For if we deliberately keep on sinning after receiving the knowledge of the truth, no further sacrifice for sins is left for us, but only a certain fearful expectation of judgment and *a fury of fire that will consume God's enemies.* Someone who rejected the law of Moses was put to death without mercy *on the testimony of two or three witnesses.* How much greater punishment do you think that person deserves who has contempt for the Son of God, and profanes the blood of the covenant that made him holy, and insults the Spirit of grace? For we know the one who said, "*Vengeance is mine, I will repay,*" and again, "*The Lord will judge his people.*" It is a terrifying thing to fall into the hands of the living God.

But remember the former days when you endured a harsh conflict of suffering after you were enlightened. At times you were publicly exposed to abuse and afflictions, and at other times you came to share with others who were treated in that way. For in fact you shared the sufferings of those in prison, and you accepted the confiscation of your belongings with joy, because you knew that you certainly had a better and lasting possession. So do not throw away your confidence, because it has great reward. For you need endurance in order to do God's will and so receive what is promised. For *just a little longer* and *he who is coming will arrive and not delay. But my righteous one will live by faith, and if he shrinks back, I take no pleasure in him.* But we are not among those who shrink back and thus perish, but are among those who have faith and preserve their souls.

CHAPTER 11

PEOPLE COMMENDED FOR THEIR FAITH

Now faith is being sure of what we hope for, being convinced of what we do not see. For by it the people of old received God's commendation. By faith we understand that the worlds were set in order at God's command, so that the visible has its origin in the invisible. By faith Abel offered God a greater sacrifice than Cain, and through his faith he was commended as righteous because God commended him for his offerings. And through his faith he still speaks, though he is dead. By faith Enoch was taken up so that he did not see death, and he was not to be found because God took him up. For before his removal he had been commended as having pleased God. Now without faith it is impossible to please him, for the one who approaches God must believe that he exists and that he rewards those who seek him. By faith Noah, when he was warned about things not yet seen, with reverent regard constructed an ark for the deliverance of his family. Through faith he condemned the world and became an heir of the righteousness that comes by faith.

By faith Abraham obeyed when he was called to go out to a place he would later receive as an inheritance, and he went out without understanding where he was going. By faith he lived as a foreigner in the promised land as though it were a foreign country, living in tents with Isaac and Jacob, who were fellow heirs of the same promise. For he was looking forward to the city with firm foundations, whose architect and builder is God. By faith, even though Sarah herself was barren and he was too old, he received the ability to procreate because he regarded the one who had given the promise to be trustworthy. So in fact children were fathered by one man—and this one as good as dead—*like the number of stars in the sky and like the innumerable grains of sand on the seashore.* These all died in faith without receiving the things promised, but they saw them in the distance and welcomed them and acknowledged that they were strangers and foreigners on the earth. For those who speak in such a way make it clear that they are seeking a homeland. In fact, if they had been thinking of the land that they had left, they would have had opportunity to return. But as it is, they aspire to a better land, that is, a heavenly one. Therefore, God is not ashamed to be called their God, for he has prepared a city for them. By faith Abraham, when he was tested, offered up Isaac. He had received the promises, yet he was ready to offer up his only son. God had told him, *"Through Isaac descendants will carry on your name,"* and he reasoned that God could even raise him from the dead, and in a sense he received him back from there. By faith also Isaac blessed Jacob and Esau concerning the future. By faith Jacob, as he was dying, blessed each of the sons of Joseph and *worshiped as he leaned on his staff.* By faith Joseph, at the end of his life, mentioned the exodus of the sons of Israel and gave instructions about his burial.

By faith, when Moses was born, his parents hid him for three months because they saw the child was beautiful and they were not afraid of the king's edict. By faith, when he grew up, Moses refused to be called the son of Pharaoh's daughter, choosing rather to be ill-treated with the people of God than to enjoy sin's fleeting pleasure. He regarded abuse suffered for Christ to be greater wealth than the treasures of Egypt, for his eyes were fixed on the reward. By faith he left Egypt without fearing the king's anger, for he persevered as though he could see the one who is invisible. By faith he kept the Passover and the sprinkling of the blood, so that the one who destroyed the firstborn would not touch them. By faith they crossed the Red Sea as if on dry ground, but when the Egyptians tried it, they were swallowed up. By faith the walls of Jericho fell after the people marched around them for seven days. By faith Rahab the prostitute escaped the destruction of the disobedient because she welcomed the spies in peace.

And what more shall I say? For time will fail me if I tell of Gideon, Barak, Samson, Jephthah, of David and Samuel and the prophets. Through faith they conquered kingdoms, administered justice, gained what was promised, shut the mouths of lions, quenched raging fire, escaped the edge of the sword, gained strength in weakness, became mighty in battle, put foreign armies to flight, and women received back their dead raised to life. But others were tortured, not accepting release, to obtain resurrection to a better life. And others experienced mocking and flogging, and even chains and imprisonment. They were stoned, sawed apart, murdered with the sword; they went about in sheepskins and goatskins; they were destitute, afflicted, ill-treated (the world was not worthy of them); they wandered in deserts and mountains and caves and openings in the earth. And these all were commended for their faith, yet they did not receive what was promised. For God had provided something better for us, so that they would be made perfect together with us.

CHAPTER 12

THE LORD'S DISCIPLINE

Therefore, since we are surrounded by such a great cloud of witnesses, we must get rid of every weight and the sin that clings so closely, and run with endurance the race set out for us, keeping our eyes fixed on Jesus, the pioneer and perfecter of our faith. For the joy set out for him he endured the cross, disregarding its shame, and *has taken his seat at the right hand of the throne* of God. Think of him who endured such opposition against himself by sinners, so that you may not grow weary in your souls and give up. You have not yet resisted to the point of bloodshed in your struggle against sin. And have you forgotten the exhortation addressed to you as sons?

"My son, do not scorn the Lord's discipline or give up when he corrects you.
For the Lord disciplines the one he loves and chastises every son he accepts."

Endure your suffering as discipline; God is treating you as sons. For what son is there that a father does not discipline? But if you do not experience discipline, something all sons have shared in, then you are illegitimate and are not sons. Besides, we have experienced discipline from our earthly fathers and we respected them; shall we not submit ourselves all the more to the Father of spirits and receive life? For they disciplined us for a little while as seemed good to them, but he does so for our benefit, that we may share his holiness. Now all discipline seems painful at the time, not joyful. But later it produces the fruit of peace and righteousness for those trained by it. Therefore, *strengthen your listless hands and your weak knees,* and *make straight paths for your feet,* so that what is lame may not be put out of joint but be healed.

DO NOT REJECT GOD'S WARNING

Pursue peace with everyone, and holiness, for without it no one will see the Lord. See to it that no one comes short of the grace of God, that no one be like *a bitter root springing up* and causing trouble, and through it many become defiled. And see to it that no one becomes an immoral or godless person like Esau, who *sold his own birthright for a single meal.* For you know that later when he wanted to inherit the blessing, he was rejected, for he found no opportunity for repentance, although he sought the blessing with tears. For you have not come to something that can be touched, to a burning fire and darkness and gloom and a whirlwind and the blast of a trumpet and a voice uttering words such that those who heard begged to hear no more. For they could not bear what was commanded: *"If even an animal touches the mountain, it must be stoned."* In fact, the scene was so terrifying that Moses said, *"I shudder with fear."* But you have come to Mount Zion, the city of the living God, the heavenly Jerusalem, and to myriads of angels, to the assembly and congregation of the first-born, who are enrolled in heaven, and to God, the judge of all, and to the spirits of the righteous, who have been made perfect, and to Jesus, the mediator of a new covenant, and to the sprinkled blood that speaks of something better than Abel's does.

Take care not to refuse the one who is speaking! For if they did not escape when they refused the one who warned them on earth, how much less shall we, if we reject the one who warns from heaven? Then his voice shook the earth, but now he has promised,

"*I will once more shake not only the earth but heaven too.*" Now this phrase "*once more*" indicates the removal of what is shaken, that is, of created things, so that what is unshaken may remain. So since we are receiving an unshakable kingdom, let us give thanks, and through this let us offer worship pleasing to God in devotion and awe. For our *God is indeed a devouring fire.*

CHAPTER 13

FINAL EXHORTATIONS

Brotherly love must continue. Do not neglect hospitality because through it some have entertained angels without knowing it. Remember those in prison as though you were in prison with them, and those ill-treated as though you, too, felt their torment. Marriage must be honored among all and the marriage bed kept undefiled, for God will judge sexually immoral people and adulterers. Your conduct must be free from the love of money, and you must be content with what you have, for he has said, "*I will never leave you and I will never abandon you.*" So we can say with confidence, "*The Lord is my helper, and I will not be afraid. What can people do to me?*" Remember your leaders, who spoke God's message to you; reflect on the outcome of their lives and imitate their faith. Jesus Christ is the same yesterday and today and forever! Do not be carried away by all sorts of strange teachings. For it is good for the heart to be strengthened by grace, not ritual meals, which have never benefited those who participated in them. We have an altar that those who serve in the tabernacle have no right to eat from. For the bodies of those animals whose blood the high priest brings into the sanctuary as an offering for sin are burned outside the camp. Therefore, to sanctify the people by his own blood, Jesus also suffered outside the camp. We must go out to him, then, outside the camp, bearing the abuse he experienced. For here we have no lasting city, but we seek the city that is to come. Through him then let us continually offer up a sacrifice of praise to God, that is, the fruit of our lips, acknowledging his name. And do not neglect to do good and to share what you have, for God is pleased with such sacrifices.

Obey your leaders and submit to them, for they keep watch over your souls and will give an account for their work. Let them do this with joy and not with complaints, for this would be no advantage for you. Pray for us, for we are sure that we have a clear conscience and desire to conduct ourselves rightly in every respect. I especially ask you to pray that I may be restored to you very soon.

BENEDICTION AND CONCLUSION

Now may the God of peace who by the blood of the eternal covenant brought back from the dead the great shepherd of the sheep, our

Lord Jesus, equip you with every good thing to do his will, working in us what is pleasing before him through Jesus Christ, to whom be glory forever. Amen.

Now I urge you, brothers and sisters, bear with my message of exhortation, for in fact I have written to you briefly. You should know that our brother Timothy has been released. If he comes soon, he will be with me when I see you. Greetings to all your leaders and all the saints. Those from Italy send you greetings. Grace be with you all.

JAMES

PROLOGUE

Imagine your older brother begins to tell everyone that he is God, the one who has come to bring salvation to the world. He tells your neighbors. Your friends. Your relatives. You used to play together. Now, every time he opens his mouth, you cringe in embarrassment. You have become *that* family.

This was the story of James, one of Jesus' half brothers. James had wanted nothing to do with Jesus during his time of ministry. But he didn't just reject Jesus' claims, he ridiculed him. All of that changed, however, when Jesus came back from the dead. After the crucifixion, Jesus' lifeless body had been placed in a tomb. There was no question that he was dead. But then Jesus appeared to James. And in that moment, mocking gave way to faith.

James became a leader in the church. Most of his fellow believers were Jews, raised to believe that a person had to earn God's acceptance. But Jesus' message was different. Jesus taught that God's acceptance came as a gift. All a person had to do was believe.

Some, however, took this liberating message

too far. They claimed faith in Jesus but lived no differently because of it. James had to respond to this mistake. He had to help them see that their ultimate problem was not anything they did but rather what they believed.

CHAPTER 1

SALUTATION

From James, a slave of God and the Lord Jesus Christ, to the 12 tribes dispersed abroad. Greetings!

JOY IN TRIALS

My brothers and sisters, consider it nothing but joy when you fall into all sorts of trials, because you know that the testing of your faith produces endurance. And let endurance have its perfect effect, so that you will be perfect and complete, not deficient in anything. But if anyone is deficient in wisdom, he should ask God, who gives to all generously and without reprimand, and it will be given to him. But he must ask in faith without doubting, for the one who doubts is like a wave of the sea, blown and tossed around by the wind. For that person must not suppose that he will receive anything from the Lord, since he is a double-minded individual, unstable in all his ways.

Now the believer of humble means should take pride in his high position. But the rich person's pride should be in his humiliation because he will pass away like a wildflower in the meadow. For the sun rises with its heat and dries up the meadow; the petal of the flower falls off and its beauty is lost forever. So also the rich person in the midst of his pursuits will wither away. Happy is the one who endures testing because when he has proven to be genuine, he will receive the crown of life that God promised to those who love him. Let no one say when he is tempted, "I am tempted by God," for God cannot be tempted by evil, and he himself tempts no one. But each one is tempted when he is lured and enticed by his own desires. Then when desire conceives, it gives birth to sin, and when sin is full grown, it gives birth to death. Do not be led astray, my dear brothers and sisters. All generous giving and every perfect gift is from above, coming down from the Father of lights, with whom there is no variation or the slightest hint of change. By his sovereign plan he gave us birth through the message of truth, that we would be a kind of firstfruits of all he created.

LIVING OUT THE MESSAGE

Understand this, my dear brothers and sisters! Let every person be quick to listen, slow to speak, slow to anger. For human anger does not accomplish God's righteousness. So put away all filth and evil excess and humbly welcome the message implanted within you, which is able to save your souls. But be sure you live out the message and do not merely listen to it and so deceive yourselves. For if someone merely listens to the message and does not live it out, he is like someone who gazes at his own face in a mirror. For he gazes at himself and then goes out and immediately forgets what sort of person he was. But the one who peers into the perfect law of liberty and fixes his attention there, and does not become a forgetful listener but one who lives it out—he will be blessed in what he does. If someone thinks he is religious yet does not bridle his tongue, and so deceives his heart, his religion is futile. Pure and undefiled religion before God the Father is this: to care for orphans and widows in their adversity and to keep oneself unstained by the world.

CHAPTER 2

PREJUDICE AND THE LAW OF LOVE

My brothers and sisters, do not show prejudice if you possess faith in our glorious Lord Jesus Christ. For if someone comes into your assembly wearing a gold ring and fine clothing, and a poor person enters in filthy clothes, do you pay attention to the one who is finely dressed and say, "You sit here in a good place," and to the poor person, "You stand over there," or "Sit on the floor"? If so, have you not made distinctions among yourselves and become judges with evil motives? Listen, my dear brothers and sisters! Did not God choose the poor in the world to be rich in faith and heirs of the kingdom that he promised to those who love him? But you have dishonored the poor! Are not the rich oppressing you and dragging you into the courts? Do they not blaspheme the good name of the one you belong to? But if you fulfill the royal law as expressed in this scripture, "*You shall love your neighbor as yourself,*" you are doing well. But if you show prejudice, you are committing sin and are convicted by the law as violators. For the one who obeys the whole law but fails in one point has become guilty of all of it. For he who said, "*Do not commit adultery,*" also said, "*Do not murder.*" Now if you do not commit adultery but do commit murder, you have become a violator of the law. Speak and act as those who will be judged by a law that gives freedom. For judgment is merciless for the one who has shown no mercy. But mercy triumphs over judgment.

FAITH AND WORKS TOGETHER

What good is it, my brothers and sisters, if someone claims to have faith but does not have works? Can this kind of faith save him? If a brother or sister is poorly clothed and lacks daily food, and one of you says to them, "Go in peace, keep warm and eat well," but you do not give them what the body needs, what good is it? So also faith, if it does not have works, is dead being by itself. But someone will say, "You have faith and I have works." Show me your faith without works and I will show you faith by my works. You believe that God is one; well and good. Even the demons believe that—and tremble with fear.

But would you like evidence, you empty fellow, that faith without works is useless? Was not Abraham our father justified by works when he offered Isaac his son on the altar? You see that his faith was working together with his works and his faith was perfected by works. And the scripture was fulfilled that says, **"Now Abraham believed God and it was counted to him for righteousness,"** and *he was called God's friend.* You see that a person is justified by works and not by faith alone. And similarly, was not Rahab the prostitute also justified by works when she welcomed the messengers and sent them out by another way? For just as the body without the spirit is dead, so also faith without works is dead.

CHAPTER 3

THE POWER OF THE TONGUE

Not many of you should become teachers, my brothers and sisters, because you know that we will be judged more strictly. For we all stumble in many ways. If someone does not stumble in what he says, he is a perfect individual, able to control the entire body as well. And if we put bits into the mouths of horses to get them to obey us, then we guide their entire bodies. Look at ships too: Though they are so large and driven by harsh winds, they are steered by a tiny rudder wherever the pilot's inclination directs. So, too, the tongue is a small part of the body, yet it has great pretensions. Think how small a flame sets a huge forest ablaze. And the tongue is a fire! The tongue represents the world of wrongdoing among the parts of our bodies. It pollutes the entire body and sets fire to the course of human existence—and is set on fire by hell.

For every kind of animal, bird, reptile, and sea creature is subdued and has been subdued by humankind. But no human being can subdue the tongue; it is a restless evil, full of deadly poison. With it we bless the Lord and Father, and with it we curse people made in God's image. From the same mouth come blessing and cursing. These things should not be so, my brothers and sisters. A spring does not pour out fresh water and bitter water from the same opening, does it? Can a fig tree produce olives, my brothers and sisters, or a vine produce figs? Neither can a salt water spring produce fresh water.

TRUE WISDOM

Who is wise and understanding among you? By his good conduct he should show his works done in the gentleness that wisdom brings.

But if you have bitter jealousy and selfishness in your hearts, do not boast and tell lies against the truth. Such wisdom does not come from above but is earthly, natural, demonic. For where there is jealousy and selfishness, there is disorder and every evil practice. But the wisdom from above is first pure, then peaceable, gentle, accommodating, full of mercy and good fruit, impartial, and not hypocritical. And the fruit that consists of righteousness is planted in peace among those who make peace.

CHAPTER 4

PASSIONS AND PRIDE

Where do the conflicts and where do the quarrels among you come from? Is it not from this, from your passions that battle inside you? You desire and you do not have; you murder and envy and you cannot obtain; you quarrel and fight. You do not have because you do not ask; you ask and do not receive because you ask wrongly, so you can spend it on your passions.

Adulterers, do you not know that friendship with the world means hostility toward God? So whoever decides to be the world's friend makes himself God's enemy. Or do you think the scripture means nothing when it says, "The spirit that God caused to live within us has an envious yearning"? But he gives greater grace. Therefore it says, "**God opposes the proud, but he gives grace to the humble.**" So submit to God. But resist the devil and he will flee from you. Draw near to God and he will draw near to you. Cleanse your hands, you sinners, and make your hearts pure, you double-minded. Grieve, mourn, and weep. Turn your laughter into mourning and your joy into despair. Humble yourselves before the Lord and he will exalt you.

Do not speak against one another, brothers and sisters. He who speaks against a fellow believer or judges a fellow believer speaks against the law and judges the law. But if you judge the law, you are not a doer of the law but its judge. But there is only one who is lawgiver and judge—the one who is able to save and destroy. On the other hand, who are you to judge your neighbor?

Come now, you who say, "Today or tomorrow we will go into this or that town and spend a year there and do business and make a profit." You do not know about tomorrow. What is your life like? For you are a puff of smoke that appears for a short time and then vanishes. You ought to say instead, "If the Lord is willing, then we will live and do this or that." But as it is, you boast about your arrogant plans. All such boasting is evil. So whoever knows what is good to do and does not do it is guilty of sin.

CHAPTER 5

WARNING TO THE RICH

Come now, you rich! Weep and cry aloud over the miseries that are coming on you. Your riches have rotted and your clothing has become moth-eaten. Your gold and silver have rusted and their rust will be a witness against you. It will consume your flesh like fire. It is in the last days that you have hoarded treasure! Look, the pay you have held back from the workers who mowed your fields cries out against you, and the cries of the reapers have reached the ears of the Lord of Heaven's Armies. You have lived indulgently and luxuriously on the earth. You have fattened your hearts in a day of slaughter. You have condemned and murdered the righteous person, although he does not resist you.

PATIENCE IN SUFFERING

So be patient, brothers and sisters, until the Lord's return. Think of how the farmer waits for the precious fruit of the ground and is patient for it until it receives the early and late rains. You also be patient and strengthen your hearts, for the Lord's return is near. Do not grumble against one another, brothers and sisters, so that you may not be judged. See, the judge stands before the gates! As an example of suffering and patience, brothers and sisters, take the prophets who spoke in the Lord's name. Think of how we regard as blessed those who have endured. You have heard of Job's endurance and you have seen the Lord's purpose, that *the Lord is full of compassion and mercy*. And above all, my brothers and sisters, do not swear, either by heaven or by earth or by any other oath. But let your "Yes" be yes and your "No" be no, so that you may not fall into judgment.

PRAYER FOR THE SICK

Is anyone among you suffering? He should pray. Is anyone in good spirits? He should sing praises. Is anyone among you ill? He should summon the elders of the church, and they should pray for him and anoint him with olive oil in the name of the Lord. And the prayer of faith will save the one who is sick and the Lord will raise him up—and if he has committed sins, he will be forgiven. So confess your sins to one another and pray for one another so that you may be healed. The prayer of a righteous person has great effectiveness. Elijah was a human being like us, and he prayed earnestly that it would not rain and there was no rain on the land for three years and six months! Then he prayed again, and the sky gave rain and the land sprouted with a harvest.

My brothers and sisters, if anyone among you wanders from the truth and someone turns him back, he should know that the one who turns a sinner back from his wandering path will save that person's soul from death and will cover a multitude of sins.

JUDE

PROLOGUE

Sometimes it is difficult to see what, or who, is right in front of you. This was the problem for Jude, one of Jesus' half brothers. Jude grew up with Jesus and had a front-row seat to hear his teachings and see his miracles. Despite all of that, Jude failed to believe that Jesus was who he claimed to be . . . until the resurrection. When Jesus rose from the dead, everything changed, including Jesus' little brother. Jude transformed from a vocal critic to a committed follower of Jesus. He was all in.

Imagine, then, how Jude felt when he heard that some false teachers were spreading throughout the church. These teachers taught that the physical world didn't matter—only the spiritual one was important. And if the world didn't matter, then how believers lived in that world didn't matter either. In short, believers could live however they wanted.

Jude's response was quick and clear. The threat was serious. The church had to act. There was one critical thing it had to do.

CHAPTER 1

SALUTATION

From Jude, a slave of Jesus Christ and brother of James, to those who are called, wrapped in the love of God the Father and kept for Jesus Christ. May mercy, peace, and love be lavished on you!

CONDEMNATION OF THE FALSE TEACHERS

Dear friends, although I have been eager to write to you about our common salvation, I now feel compelled instead to write to encourage you to contend earnestly for the faith that was once for all entrusted to the saints. For certain men have secretly slipped in among you—men who long ago were marked out for the condemnation I am about to describe—ungodly men who have turned the grace of our God into a license for evil and who deny our only Master and Lord, Jesus Christ.

Now I desire to remind you (even though you have been fully informed of these facts once for all) that Jesus, having saved the people out of the land of Egypt, later destroyed those who did not believe. You also know that the angels who did not keep within their proper domain but abandoned their own place of residence, he has kept in eternal chains in utter darkness, locked up for the judgment of the great Day. So also Sodom and Gomorrah and the neighboring towns, since they indulged in sexual immorality and pursued unnatural desire in a way similar to these angels, are now displayed as an example by suffering the punishment of eternal fire.

Yet these men, as a result of their dreams, defile the flesh, reject authority, and insult the glorious ones. But even when Michael the archangel was arguing with the devil and debating with him concerning Moses' body, he did not dare to bring a slanderous judgment, but said, "May the Lord rebuke you!" But these men do not understand the things they slander, and they are being destroyed by the very things that, like irrational animals, they instinctively comprehend. Woe to them! For they have traveled down Cain's path, and because of greed have abandoned themselves to Balaam's error; hence, they will certainly perish in Korah's rebellion. These men are dangerous reefs at your love feasts, feasting without reverence, feeding only themselves. They are waterless clouds, carried along by the winds; autumn trees without fruit—twice dead, uprooted; wild sea waves, spewing out the foam of their shame; wayward stars for whom the utter depths of eternal darkness have been reserved.

Now Enoch, the seventh in descent beginning with Adam, even prophesied of them, saying, "Look! The Lord is coming with thousands and thousands of his holy ones, to execute judgment on all, and to convict every person of all their thoroughly ungodly deeds that they have committed, and of all the harsh words that ungodly sinners have spoken against him." These people are grumblers and fault-finders who go wherever their desires lead them, and they give bombastic speeches, enchanting folks for their own gain.

EXHORTATION TO THE FAITHFUL

But you, dear friends—recall the predictions foretold by the apostles of our Lord Jesus Christ. For they said to you, "At the end of time there will come scoffers, propelled by their own ungodly desires." These people are divisive, worldly, devoid of the Spirit. But you, dear friends, by building yourselves up in your most holy faith, by praying in the Holy Spirit, maintain yourselves in the love of God while anticipating the mercy of our Lord Jesus Christ that brings eternal life. And have mercy on those who waver; save others by snatching them out of the fire; have mercy on others, coupled with a fear of God, hating even the clothes stained by the flesh.

FINAL BLESSING

Now to the one who is able to keep you from falling, and to cause you to stand, rejoicing, without blemish before his glorious presence, to the only God our Savior through Jesus Christ our Lord, be glory, majesty, power, and authority, before all time, and now, and for all eternity. Amen.